She and Chance had made a baby.

As far as Alexa was concerned, it was a tiny miracle.

A miracle she needed to share. Swallowing against the lump in her throat, she whispered, "Chance..."

"I think you said everything you needed to say during our last phone call."

Goodbye was pretty much all they'd said during that phone call, and so much had happened since then. Finding out that she was pregnant, the bombing, the reports of his death.

He started to turn away, then stopped. Alexa's heart jumped to her throat as he reached his hand and brushed his fingers through h   A muscle in his jaw clenched, and she   plessly into the firestorm   t eyes.

For a split   to pull her closer, t   neath the sparkling   ng ballroom. To kiss her th   ery night since in her dreams.

His voice gravel rough, he said, "I think you must have dropped this."

Only after he moved away from her did she lift a hand to the spot above her ear. Her fingers brushed against a thin piece of metal. She pulled the hairpin from her hair and stared at the bejeweled butterfly clip she hadn't seen in four months.

* * *

HILLCREST HOUSE: Destination...romance

Dear Reader,

Welcome back to Hillcrest House: destination... romance!

What is your earliest childhood memory? While I think I remember going to the hospital after my younger brother was born, I was only three at the time, so I'm not sure if that's a real memory or not. I definitely remember the day of my fifth birthday. I can still picture waking up, seeing the sunlight streaming through the curtains and thinking to myself, "It's my birthday today, and I'm FIVE!"

For Chance McClaren and Alexa Mayhew, some of their early memories aren't happy ones. Chance suffered a traumatic injury as a child and Alexa lost her parents. Their reactions to these incidents have shaped their lives in very different ways—Chance is a risk-taker and adventurer; Alexa is careful, always playing things safe.

But when a weekend fling between these two opposites leads to a plus sign on a pregnancy test, will they be willing to put their pasts behind them and place their hope in a future together?

I hope you enjoy this return to Hillcrest House and that you will look for cousin Evie McClaren's book, coming soon! These couples might not be looking for love, but at a gorgeous Victorian hotel that promises romance and happily-ever-after, what else can they say but "I do"?

Happy reading!

Stacy Connelly

How to Be a Blissful Bride

Stacy Connelly

Recycling programs
for this product may
not exist in your area.

ISBN-13: 978-1-335-46600-6

How to Be a Blissful Bride

Copyright © 2018 by Stacy Cornell

This edition published by arrangement with Harlequin Books S.A.

For questions and comments about the quality of this book, please contact us at CustomerService@Harlequin.com.

Printed in U.S.A.

www.Harlequin.com

Stacy Connelly has dreamed of publishing books since she was a kid, writing stories about a girl and her horse. Eventually, boys made it onto the pages as she discovered a love of romance and the promise of happily-ever-after. When she is not lost in the land of make-believe, Stacy lives in Arizona with her three spoiled dogs. She loves to hear from readers at stacyconnelly@cox.net or stacyconnelly.com.

Books by Stacy Connelly

Harlequin Special Edition

Hillcrest House

The Best Man Takes a Bride

The Pirelli Brothers

His Secret Son
Romancing the Rancher
Small-Town Cinderella
Daddy Says, "I Do!"
Darcy and the Single Dad
Her Fill-In Fiancé

Temporary Boss...Forever Husband
The Wedding She Always Wanted
Once Upon a Wedding
All She Wants for Christmas

Visit the Author Profile page
at Harlequin.com for more titles.

To Cindy—

So glad our love of romance
(and especially of Special Edition)
has brought us together as friends and fellow writers!

Chapter One

Chance McClaren took a deep breath of cool, ocean-scented air and willed his body to relax. Closing his eyes, he let the sound of the waves rushing against the rocky shoreline wash over him. Faint sunlight barely broke through the November haze, but he focused on the warmth against his skin. Gradually, his muscles started to relax. Neck, shoulders, arms. Not his right leg, but that tightness was due to more than tension.

He could do this. He could smile, he could play along. He could pretend…for as long as it took for his body to heal. For as long as it took to get the hell out of Clearville.

Opening his eyes, he hazarded a glance over his shoulder and scowled. The old lady was still there. Hovering over him. Staring down at him. Watching him.

Turning at the waist until the joints in his back popped, Chance muttered, "You're losin' it, man."

He rubbed at the back of his neck, the skin there feeling bare without the weight of the familiar camera strap. As a photojournalist, Chance had the gift of capturing a moment for everyone to see. Of making still images come alive for people half a world away.

But bringing life to a photo was one thing. Imagining that his family's Victorian hotel, the old lady behind him, was living, breathing, watching him... That was something else.

"Please come, Chance," his younger sister, Rory, had pleaded. "You haven't been to Hillcrest House in years. Being here will be good for you."

His sister had always loved the old gal. Chance's lips twitched in a smile. The hotel *and* their Aunt Evelyn, who ran the place and would slay him with a killer glare for even thinking of her as old.

Rory and their cousin, Evie, had moved to Clearville months earlier to take over while their aunt went through cancer treatments. Aunt Evelyn was splitting time between staying with his parents and staying with Evie's parents as she recovered from surgeries and chemotherapy.

Even if they hadn't had their hands full, Chance couldn't have stayed at his parents' house for another minute. He loved them, he did. But the worry and the lingering sorrow in their gazes, even now that they knew he was safe—knew he was *alive*—weighed down on him. Suffocated him.

They'd never understood his desire to see the world, to live his life with his backpack and camera gear the only baggage allowed. He was free to come and go as he pleased, to live his life the way he wanted, and his work made a difference! He had contacts around the globe. He could go into places other journalists couldn't go and tell the stories that might otherwise remain unheard.

His parents had always had a straighter, safer path in mind for him. One that included following in his father's footsteps and taking over the small photography studio

Matthew McClaren owned, buying a house and settling down with a wife and kids.

Chance had jumped the curb and taken his life off-road when he left home at eighteen and had never come close to veering anywhere near that white-picket-fence neighborhood again. He wasn't the settling kind, and while his parents might not understand that, Chance always believed they respected what he'd accomplished, respected the heights he'd achieved in his career...

Or at least he had until that whispered conversation he'd overheard, the one that made it clear he couldn't stay under his parents' roof any longer than necessary.

We're your family, Chance. We love you.

His mother's words, the confusion on her face when he walked out—first as a hotheaded kid and then again, just a few weeks ago—cut deep. But he'd known if he didn't leave, he would only end up saying something he would regret.

His parents hadn't wanted him to be alone while he was recovering, and he'd thought staying with Rory and Evie might be enough to ease their concern while still giving him space to breathe.

Now he wasn't so sure.

"Oh, Chance, this will be so perfect!" his sister had gushed the moment he set foot inside the family hotel. "Our current photographer is moving away soon."

He'd forgotten about the whole all-inclusive wedding destination business that had been his aunt's brainchild about a year ago. He didn't know how considering, as the hotel's wedding coordinator, the ceremonies were all Rory talked about. Especially now that she'd found a groom-to-be of her own.

"You can fill in while you're here!"

Wedding photographer? Yeah, that was right up there

with fashion photographer as a worst nightmare. "Not exactly my thing, Rory."

He felt like he'd kicked a puppy as he watched the excitement in his little sister's eyes dim. Jamison Porter, Rory's fiancé, had studied him carefully during that first meeting and suggested, "Why don't you let your brother get settled before offering him a job, sweetheart?"

At that, Rory had recovered quickly, wrapping her arms around him in a far more cautious version of her usual exuberant hug. "Of course! What was I thinking? We have the cottage house set up for you."

The caretaker's cottage was a small wood and stone structure on the grounds, but well away from the hotel itself. Chance welcomed the privacy even if staying there felt like living in a very girlie dollhouse thanks to Rory's decorating skills.

But he'd take the dollhouse over his childhood bedroom. And it was only for a month—maybe two. His leg was getting stronger every day, and Chance refused to think he wouldn't make it back to 100 percent.

And after a few days of consideration, he'd even agreed to fill in as wedding photographer—which he still couldn't quite believe. But he needed something to keep his mind active, to keep moving.

He'd traveled to some of the most desperate, poverty-stricken, war-torn areas in the world and yet nothing—nothing—was quite as scary as walking into a room filled with marriage-minded women riding high on romance.

Shuddering, he shifted his weight to his right side, testing his leg without the help of the crutches he'd only recently left behind. Sharp shards of pain sliced through muscle and bone. He'd pushed himself too hard, the packed sand more of a challenge than he'd expected. He had a long walk back to the hotel in front of him.

He pulled in a breath before taking that first step, beads of sweat popping up along his hairline and instantly cooling in the ocean breeze. The stormy blue-gray water was nearly the same color as the stormy blue-gray sky. Nearly the same color as a pair of stormy blue-gray eyes that had haunted him for months.

Alexa Mayhew had been draped in gold the night they met. Beneath a sparkling crystal chandelier, she'd glittered with the grace and elegance of a goddess. She was tall and slender, with a poise and prestige that allowed her to move in elite circles where most mortals wouldn't be welcomed. And yet he'd sensed a restlessness inside her the moment their gazes met across the ballroom, a need to throw aside the fake smiles and polite facade and grab hold of something real...

Or so he'd thought until she made herself clear. She'd been slumming their weekend together. Different worlds, different lives...different bank accounts.

Reaching into the pocket of his baggy khakis, he fingered the small jeweled hairpin he'd been carrying with him since that weekend. In his line of work, he'd learned to travel light. No extra baggage allowed. And yet, he hadn't been able to leave the small reminder behind any more than he could convince himself to return it to the woman it belonged to. Such a small thing, he hadn't thought carrying it with him could hurt.

He'd certainly never imagined it would save his life.

He wasn't superstitious and he wasn't sentimental. He certainly didn't believe in love at first sight, so why was he having such a hard time letting Alexa go?

"Welcome to Hillcrest. And I understand congratulations are in order?"

Standing in the elegant lobby of the Victorian hotel,

Alexa Mayhew hoped she managed a smile to fool the bright-eyed wedding coordinator.

"It's not official yet," she murmured, trying to somewhat inconspicuously hide her left hand in the folds of her wide-legged gray trousers. Her naked left hand, unlike the woman in front of her who sported a sparkling rock on her own third finger.

"But we'd still like a tour of the grounds while we're staying here if that's possible." Griffin James wrapped an arm around Alexa's shoulders and pulled her tight to his side. "Isn't that right, sweetie?"

Alexa stumbled slightly at the sudden move before regaining her balance. She and Griffin had checked in earlier that day after a long drive from Los Angeles. Worn out from hours in the car and feeling more than a little nauseous from the twists and turns on the mountain roads leading into the small Northern California town, she had lain down for a short rest while Griffin had—

Alexa tried to withhold a sigh. Who knows what Griffin had done? Announced their impending engagement from the top turret of the towering Victorian mansion, for all she knew.

She shot her could-be fiancé a glare he returned with a wink and a grin, knowing she could never stay mad at him. He'd been her best friend since childhood, the one person she could turn to when times got tough. The one person who could always make her laugh—which was pretty much what she'd done when he proposed.

"Griffin," she started to protest.

"Come on. It'll be fun. A good chance to take a look around." His eyebrows rose pointedly, reminding her why he had chosen this particular hotel.

Alexa hadn't really cared where they stayed, too eager to accept his offer of a break away from the demands of her grandmother's charity foundation. And from the demands of her grandmother.

From the time she'd gone to live with Virginia Mayhew, the wealthy philanthropist had instilled in Alexa a sense of responsibility. In the past decade or so, she had become the face of the foundation. She spent countless hours fund-raising, overseeing charity events, speaking with the media, all in an effort to give back.

But for the first time in her life, Alexa had something she wanted to hold on to…just for herself. She needed to get away, and though she was aware of the faint and almost constant vibrations coming from the cell phone tucked in her purse, she refused to check the barrage of emails and text messages.

Understanding Griffin's unspoken professional interest in looking around the hotel, she said, "We'd love a tour."

"I have some time free now if you're not too tired from traveling," the woman offered. "And I'm Rory, by the way. Rory Mc—"

A high-pitched whistle sounded, and she glanced at the phone in her own hand. A dreamy smile lit her already beautiful face at the text flashing across the screen. The moment lasted only a split second before she appeared to snap back to reality. A slight blush rose to her cheeks as she slipped the phone into a hidden pocket in the folds of her full skirt. "Sorry about that. That was *my* fiancé and… Well—" she shot a woman-to-woman look at Alexa "—you know how it is, right?"

"Of course." Even as happy as the other woman looked, Alexa would bet Rory hadn't laughed out loud when her fiancé proposed.

"Let's start inside, and then I can show you around the grounds. We remodeled the gazebo over the summer, and it's always a popular spot—depending on the time of year for the ceremony. Have the two of you picked a date yet?" Rory asked.

Griffin shot Alexa a questioning look, calling her out on dragging her feet—literally across the richly patterned carpet and in giving a definitive answer to the question he'd asked.

Fall decorations highlighted the elegant lobby—a cornucopia on the concierge desk; red, yellow and orange leaf garland wrapped the deep walnut carved columns, and a huge grapevine wreath dotted with tiny pumpkins and squash hung above the river-stone fireplace in the sitting area. Scents of cinnamon and cloves filled the air.

All signs of how quickly time was flying by. Hard to believe Thanksgiving was only three weeks away. Especially when every time Alexa closed her eyes, her thoughts drifted back to the end of summer.

"Sometime before April, I'm thinking," Griffin answered wryly when Alexa stayed silent.

"Hmm, that's not much time," the wedding coordinator warned before holding up a hand. "Not that we couldn't pull it off."

"Yeah, well, it's kind of a…predetermined time frame."

As Rory started talking about the history of the hotel, Alexa jabbed an elbow into Griffin's side. "Would you stop?" she muttered from behind her smile, voice low enough for only Griffin to hear.

"What? It's true. By April, you'll be—"

"I know. I know. But don't you feel at least a little bit guilty going through with this tour when it's doubtful we'd get married here anyway?"

"Naw, it's kinda fun." Griffin tipped his golden blond head toward the wedding coordinator. "It's like getting a tour from Snow White…"

"Behave," she warned him, though past experience told

her it would do little good. Besides, he was right. Their guide did resemble the Disney princess, but beyond that... Alexa frowned, a memory tugging at her mind like an elusive song lyric she could almost but not quite capture.

"As much as I love this place's history," Rory was saying, "it's the air of romance that brought me back here." Leaning closer, she confided, "My cousin, Evie, wouldn't like hearing me say this, but I have to tell you that Hillcrest is, well, special. People have a way of finding their own happily-ever-after here."

Griffin made a sound Alexa hoped the wedding coordinator would believe to be an indulgent laugh. "Hear that, sweetheart, our own happily-ever-after."

Alexa didn't want to think about romance in the air or happily-ever-after. For almost as long as she could remember, she had been one to play it safe. Her jet-setting parents had loved action and adventure—skiing in St. Moritz one day and sunbathing in the Bahamas the next. They'd let life take them wherever the wind had blown, sweeping in and out of her childhood like a hurricane.

After they died, her grandmother had provided Alexa with the stability she craved. No more wondering. No more worrying. No more whirlwind.

Not until that night almost four months ago when she'd hosted a fund-raiser for one of the many charities her grandmother supported. When she'd met the striking blue-eyed gaze of the most handsome man she'd ever seen. Her heart had stopped, her breath had caught and she'd been swept up in something beyond her control.

Even in that first electric connection, she'd known. There would be consequences. She couldn't cast aside years of living each day with a carefully laid out plan and then expect to pick up where she left off like nothing had happened. Not when Chance McClaren had happened.

In those first few weeks following the charity auction, he'd played constantly on her mind. Laughing and teasing her thoughts as if he'd stood right beside her, whispering in her ear. After all, he had promised he'd be in touch, and Alexa had jumped at every call, scrambled for her cell phone at every text, scoured her email every few minutes over calls and texts and emails that *weren't* from Chance.

By the time he did call, some five weeks later, she'd already come to a decision. What they'd had was a fling. Nothing more, and it was over. She'd sensed his surprise. No doubt there were dozens of women who would be thrilled to hear from him no matter how long it had been since he'd called. But in the end he'd agreed and abided by her wishes.

She hadn't heard from him again and did her best not to think of him.

Alexa told herself the mental roadblock would eventually work…right up until the moment she realized she'd missed her period. She was pregnant, the father of her child a man she barely knew. A whirlwind who'd stormed in—and out—of her life with a recklessness that left her head and heart spinning.

How was she supposed to tell a man who lived out of a backpack that he was going to be a father? Alexa had rehearsed what she would say dozens of times as she made dozens of calls, trying to reach him.

And then fate seemed to take the decision out of her hands as she woke one morning to see the headline scrolling across a national news channel.

Photojournalist Chance McClaren killed in bomb attack in Kabul.

"How long have you worked here, Rory?" Griffin asked their guide as she led them back to the lobby after show-

ing them the elegant ballroom. The hotel's old-fashioned feel filled the room from the dark, carved check-in desk, to the wall of small cubbyholes for guest messages, to an actual phone booth and its replica of an early 1900s phone.

But like any modern hotel, the lobby was a busy spot with families coming and going, bellhops pushing packed luggage carts, and employees offering advice for things to see and do in the nearby Victorian town of Clearville.

Rory stopped to allow a chatting couple to wheel by with a stroller. And as she had for the past few months, Alexa locked in on the baby strapped inside. Her breath caught at the sight. An infant with her eyes closed, her chubby cheeks pink with sleep, her head slouched to one side. So sweet, so small...

She wrapped her arms around her waist. Before she'd gotten pregnant, she hadn't understood that she wouldn't need to wait for her baby to be born to feel such a deep connection with the new life inside her. She was amazed by how much she already loved the child growing in her womb. How she loved the idea of a little boy or little girl with dark hair and startling blue eyes like—

No, she wouldn't think about the baby's father. She wouldn't.

She watched with a combination of anxiety and anticipation as the mother stopped for a moment to adjust the lacy pink sock barely clinging to the toes of the tiniest foot she'd ever seen.

"Well, I've worked here as a wedding coordinator for the past six months or so," Rory was saying, "but my family has owned the hotel for decades. My Aunt Evelyn runs the place now, but the McClarens have—"

"What—" Alexa stopped so suddenly, Griffin almost knocked her over. "What did you say your last name was?"

"McClaren." Rory's blue gaze—her familiar blue

gaze—swung back and forth between Alexa and Griffin. "Didn't I say that earlier?"

"Alexa?" Griffin's arm tightened around her shoulders as she swayed against him. "What's wrong?"

"Nothing."

Everything...

It wasn't easy to spot the resemblance between masculine, rugged features and this delicately feminine woman, but Alexa must have subconsciously noticed the similarities. The rich, almost black hair, the high, sculpted cheekbones, those blue eyes...

The thick, patterned carpet swirled beneath her feet as the room spun. "I'm not feeling very well. I think I need to lie down..."

"Of course. I'll walk you back to the suite."

To the suite. Alexa fought a hysterical laugh. That wasn't nearly far away enough to escape the dizzying thoughts whipping through her mind.

The McClaren family hotel... *Chance's* family's hotel?

And before she could make her escape, the hotel's carved entry doors opened and in walked the father of her child.

Chapter Two

At first he thought he was imagining things.

It had happened before, after the explosion. The blast that shattered his leg had also left him with a serious concussion—one that had him drifting in and out of consciousness for days. In that confused state, he'd seen Alexa at his side. Heard her voice. Smelled the honey-lilac scent of her skin.

He hadn't stopped to think that her presence made no sense. The wealthy granddaughter of one of California's biggest and most generous philanthropists might raise money for victims of war-torn countries, but she didn't travel to war-torn countries.

She certainly wouldn't have belonged in a crowded field hospital where understaffed doctors and nurses did their best to care for those injured in the series of bombings.

But he'd been so sure of her presence that he'd nearly gotten in a fight with one of the doctors once he reached semiconsciousness, unable to understand why the man refused to let him see Alexa. Why he was keeping her away when she'd been *right there*?

Later, as the uncertainty clouding his mind started to clear, he realized it had all been some kind of delusion. He'd been embarrassed to have been so fooled by his own mind. Unsettled that a woman he barely knew—a woman he'd spent no more than a weekend with and one who wanted nothing more to do with him—had been the person he'd reached for, clung to, even in such a confused state.

And so even though he'd thought of calling since he'd returned to the States, he'd purposely not picked up the phone.

Now, as the color drained from her face, he wished he had.

She looked as beautiful and ethereal now as the night they'd met. That night, she'd been wrapped in gold, her blond hair intricately woven on top of her head, her smooth bangs held in place by the jeweled butterfly hairpin. Today, she was draped in silver, her shoulder-length hair caught more sedately in a ponytail at her nape. As he watched, she hugged her arms around her waist, her blue-gray eyes huge in her gorgeous face.

"Chance—" his sister's expression brightened as she caught sight of him "—come meet two of our guests. Alexa Mayhew, Griffin James, this is my brother, Chance McClaren."

He didn't remember moving, but he suddenly stood in front of Alexa, inches away from the woman who'd been on his mind and under his skin for months. "Alexa…"

"Chance."

She reached out, her hand hovering in the air between them as if she wasn't quite sure that he was truly there, and his heart clenched. The uncertainty in her expression hit hard as he grasped her hand in his. The soft skin, the sweet scent, all of it real this time.

"Alexa," he said again, a whisper of sound beneath his breath.

"Chance. I— It's…" Her throat worked as she swallowed. "So good to meet you."

Meet him? Meet him! She'd done a damn sight more than *met* him in a hotel room in Santa Barbara almost four months ago.

Shock held him motionless, Alexa's hand still in his, until the man at her side spoke. "If you'll excuse us. Alexa isn't feeling well."

The man—Chance couldn't even recall what his sister said the guy's name was—had a protective arm wrapped around Alexa's shoulders. Chance had barely spared him a glance earlier, but summed him up now with a quick look. Wealthy, sophisticated, handsome. Someone very much a part of Alexa's world.

The swift slice cut deep, but Chance had endured worse pain. That was one lesson he could thank Lisette for. Finding his fiancée in bed with another man had cured him of any belief in love, marriage, or even whatever the hell it was he thought he and Alexa had found in a five-star hotel penthouse suite.

But cured or not, he couldn't help taking a few shots of his own. "You look so…familiar. Are you sure we haven't met somewhere before?"

"I, uh, don't think so."

"No? So we didn't meet—I don't know, parasailing along the Waterfront? Or maybe bungee jumping off the Bridge to Nowhere?" Chance wouldn't have thought it possible, but Alexa turned even paler, and he really started to feel like an ass. He stopped himself before he mentioned her last whispered wish.

Making love under the stars.

"Alexa is hardly the type to go bungee jumping," the golden boy at her side said drily.

"Maybe someday she'll have the opportunity to take that chance."

Her turbulent blue-gray eyes met his. Their gazes lingered, clung, like they had that night in Santa Barbara.

Come on, Lexi, he'd whispered, *take a chance.*

And she had. For a weekend. And no, they hadn't had time to fulfill her wild and thoroughly facetious bucket list wishes of parasailing or bungee jumping. But he'd flown high enough and fallen hard enough that for a moment he thought he could have died happily in her arms…

But it was just a moment. One weekend, and Chance had never met a woman that he couldn't forget once he moved on. Maybe that was the problem. Ever since the explosion, he hadn't been moving. Not on to a new job, not on to a new assignment, not on to a new country across the world. He was stuck. And like some kind of shark, if he didn't keep in constant motion, he couldn't breathe.

That was the only reason why his chest hurt as he gazed at Alexa.

The man by her side glanced between them before murmuring, "Something tells me that's not happening anytime soon."

Chance opened his mouth to argue like the fool he was when his cousin, Evie McClaren, spotted the group from across the lobby. "Chance, there you are. I've been looking for you."

"If you'll excuse us," Alexa murmured to Rory.

"Oh, of course. We can finish the tour later."

"Thank you for taking your time with us this afternoon."

Always so polite, always so damn proper, Chance thought with a twist of a smile that had Alexa's elegant

head lifting to an even higher angle when she caught sight of it. "Mr. McClaren."

"Ms. Mayhew... It's been a pleasure."

He drew out the word long enough for a riot of color to storm her cheeks before she turned away. Her golden boy kept his arm around her shoulders as he turned her toward the hallway leading to... Her room? His room? Theirs?

Chance shoved his hands in his pockets, fists clenched tight enough that the hairpin gouged into his palm. He didn't care about women—any one woman—enough to be jealous. Not anymore.

"Chance? Hello, Chance?"

His cousin waved a hand in front of his face to capture his attention. "Your doctor's office called about moving your therapy appointment." She gave him a stern look. "They said they tried your cell, but you weren't answering."

"Oh, Chance." Rory frowned at him, her blue eyes so similar to his own darkening in concern. "You really should have your phone with you especially when you go out by yourself."

Chance sighed. "Yes, Mom."

His cousin's arch expression wasn't nearly as concerned as his sister's. "Not your mom. Also not your secretary. Answer your own darn phone calls."

"Yes, Evie."

At the moment, the very thought of therapy exhausted him. Dammit! He used to run for miles, and now just a twenty-minute walk on the beach left him weak, winded... and in a hell of a lot of pain.

Something that must have been more obvious than he wanted to consider as Rory said, "Speaking of Mom... She says she hasn't heard from you lately and is talking about making a trip down to check on you."

Chance's jaw tightened. "You can tell her I'm fine, Ror."

"You can tell her yourself," his sister chided. "And are you so sure about that? You look…" She hesitated, biting her lower lip, her soft heart clearly worried about hurting his feelings.

"Scary," Evie interjected.

"Evie!"

"What?" His sharp-witted, sharp-tongued cousin flicked a slender hand in his direction. "He's frightening the guests. I thought that poor woman was going to faint at the sight of him."

"Oh, I don't think that was about Chance," Rory argued. "It's a big decision, you know. Choosing where to get married."

When he first woke after the explosion, a dull roar had filled his head, the pain making it almost impossible to think. With that bomb his sister dropped, a second wave hit like an aftershock.

Alexa. Married. *At Hillcrest.*

"Chance…are you sure you're okay?"

He ran a hand down his face, several day's growth of stubble scraping against his palm. "When?" he asked, his voice sounding just as rough.

"What?"

"When's the wedding?"

"Oh… Well, they haven't picked a date yet either. Why?"

"I was just wondering if I'd still be here when it happens." Hell, he needed something to make him forget about the woman. Maybe seeing Alexa marry another man would do the trick. So far nothing else had worked.

"Don't they make the cutest couple?" Rory sighed.

"Adorable." And watching them exchange vows, promising to love each other until death did them part and seal-

ing the words with a kiss… Chance's jaw locked tight. He'd just as soon stick that hairpin into his eye.

"Seriously, Chance," Evie interjected, tucking a strand of straight, chin-length hair behind one ear, "we both know I'm nowhere near as love-stupid as this one—"

"Hey!" Rory protested as their cousin waved a hand her way.

"—but if you're going to photograph the weddings around here, you need to get on board with this whole happily-ever-after crap."

"Oh, lovely," his sister muttered. "We'll be sure to put *that* in one of our brochures."

"I'm on board, Evie."

Her pointed gaze raked him from the tip of his too-long hair, to his faded to gray T-shirt, to his rumpled khakis. "Frightening the guests," she repeated.

"I'll get a haircut. And shave," he added when her look didn't change. He all but groaned, "And go shopping."

"Before this weekend?" Rory asked, catching her lower lip between her teeth once more.

"This—" He choked back a curse. This weekend was his first official Hillcrest House event.

Chance McClaren—wedding photographer.

"All right. All right. Before this weekend. You know, the two of you really should be nicer to me," he said without thinking. "After all, I almost—"

He cut himself off before he could finish the old joke, one going back to a serious injury when he was a kid. A skateboarding accident had left him in a coma followed by months of physical and occupational therapy.

Rehab had been hell, not so different from what faced him now, and he'd pushed himself as hard as he could, determined to get back to the reckless, daredevil kid he'd been before the accident. Not that he hadn't pulled out the sympathy card every chance he got.

Work his tail off to get back on a skateboard? *Sure thing.*

Pick up his dirty socks? *Come on! Didn't everyone know he was, like, seriously injured?*

But unlike in the past when Rory would meet his melodramatic statement with a give-me-a-break eye roll, this time her blue eyes filled with emotion as she said the word he hadn't. "Died, Chance." Her voice broke on his name. "You almost died."

A wave of guilt crashed over him when he thought of what his sister, his parents, his family had been through. *Not my fault*, he reminded himself, but the words didn't erase the lingering shadows from his sister's eyes whenever she looked at him.

"I'm fine, Rory. I'll be back to my old self in no time."

Reaching out, his sister squeezed his arm and gave him a sad smile. "That's what I'm afraid of."

"Rory…" His voice trailed off as she walked away, and Chance knew better than to go after her. She needed time by herself, and he wasn't sure he could catch her if he tried.

"You really are a jerk sometimes." Disdain, not sorrow, filled his cousin's icy gaze, and it was almost a relief to have Evie glaring at him. Anger he could handle, and he wondered if she was, in her own prickly way, trying to make things easier on him.

"You do realize that I had no idea what some overeager journalist was reporting. I was stuck in the hospital—"

"You were unconscious in a makeshift first-aid station half a world away."

And that is your fault, Chance. Evie didn't say the words, but he read the accusation.

"It's my job, Evie." A job he loved despite the dangers. "And you know your sister and your parents. As far as they are concerned, their job is to love you. You shouldn't make it so hard."

And then she, too, walked away, leaving him standing in the middle of the lobby with chatting guests and employees passing him on all sides. A harried businessman barked orders into his phone, jarring Chance's leg with his briefcase as he hurried by. White-hot pain seared through him, and he clenched his jaw to keep from crying out. Sweat broke out on his upper lip, and he sucked in a deep breath.

Despite what his family thought, he was not typically foolish or reckless. His job required calculated risks, but he always weighed his options before making a decision—even if he had only a split second to do so.

The smart thing to do would be to walk away. There was no payoff to be had here. No final shot to wrap up the story. No reason to slowly, painfully make his way over to the reception desk—except for one foolish, reckless urge.

He wanted to remind Alexa Mayhew that they had, indeed, met before.

"You're sure you're all right?"

Griffin had asked the same question half a dozen times since they left—escaped—the lobby for their hotel suite. He'd led her through the tiny living area with its small shades-of-blue love seat and coffee table straight to the whitewashed dining room, where he fixed her a cup of herbal tea.

She hadn't taken a sip until she was sure she could lift the mug without her hands shaking and then had to swallow a burst of hysterical laughter along with the brew. Chamomile. Did Griffin really think the soothing benefits would help in *this* situation?

Chance. Here. At Hillcrest.

The last fifteen minutes were such a blur, the moments

so surreal, she could almost believe she'd had some kind of out-of-body experience. The second she saw him, her brain had shut down even as her limbs kept going, her mouth kept moving.

Nice to meet you?

What had she been thinking? She'd been stunned, yes, but to look him in the eye and pretend they'd never met? Alexa didn't know Chance McClaren well—other than in the biblical sense—but even she had to realize a man so *macho* would take that kind of flat-out dismissal like a challenge. She didn't remember? Well, then, he would just have to remind her, wouldn't he?

Take a chance.

The play on words had been the phrase he'd used to get her out onto the dance floor, into his arms and, by the end of the evening, into his bed.

Take a chance.

Easy for him to say. He wasn't the one who'd ended up pregnant!

"Alexa?"

Jarred from her thoughts, she cupped her hands around the warm white ceramic mug and met Griffin's worried gaze. "I'm fine now. Really. I think I was just—overwhelmed for a minute back there."

He seemed to think she was referring to the tour and the wedding coordinator's ideas for their perfect wedding. He had no reason to think anything else since Alexa had never told him the name of the man she'd had that weekend fling with.

"I meant what I said, you know. Maybe it wasn't the most romantic proposal—"

"Griff—"

"But the two of us—the *three* of us—we make sense, Allie."

His offer and the sincerity in his golden gaze wrapped around her like one of his exuberant hugs. They'd met when she was eight years old—the day of her parents' funeral. Her grandmother's estate had been filled with people—inside and out. Mourners draped in black inside and paparazzi with long-lens cameras outside. She had spent most of her childhood feeling lost and alone, but she'd never felt as invisible as she had in that crowd. Neither her parents' jet-setting friends nor her grandmother's old guard seemed to have any idea what to say to a young orphan. Though she had overheard plenty of what they had to say about her...

Poor thing. What on earth do you think Virginia will do with her?

I'm sure she'll be sent to boarding school. I'm surprised Stefan and Bree hadn't enrolled her already.

To say she had slipped away unnoticed would have been a huge understatement. No one had paid attention to her when she was there; why would anyone notice when she was gone?

Alexa hadn't given much thought to where she was going. Slipping out the back entrance, she ran. For miles it had seemed, traveling that much distance before ever leaving her grandmother's property and stumbling onto the neighbor's vast estate next door.

Though the grounds were as sculpted as her grandmother's with high hedges, flower gardens and fountains, this yard had a swing set, and that was where Griffin found her.

And as if he'd come across a homeless kitten, he'd taken her back to his house, fixed her a glass of milk and a bowl of cereal. And when his mother found the two of them sometime later, Griffin had announced, "This is Alexa. Her mom and dad died, so she's gonna live with us."

She felt the same way now as she had then. Like Griffin was the one person she could count on. And she loved him. She really did. She just wished—

Alexa shook her head. Maybe that was her problem. Always wanting more than she had. The oh-so-typical poor little rich girl.

"You're my best friend, Griffin." Setting aside the mug, Alexa rounded the table to take his hands. "You have been since we were kids, and if I ever lost that, if I ever lost your friendship—"

"Not gonna happen. I promise you that. Scout's honor."

"You were so never a Boy Scout." After giving his hands a final squeeze, Alexa pushed him toward the door of their suite. "Go! You know you don't want to be stuck in this room with me."

Recently, Griffin's father had expressed an interest in Hillcrest House. Evidently, he had heard that a competing national chain had made an offer on the Victorian hotel, and he'd asked Griffin to go see whether the property was worthy enough to make a counteroffer.

Alexa was more than a little surprised Griffin had agreed. He had his own dreams that had nothing to do with becoming a hotel magnate. Dreams that could come true—if he found a way to prove himself responsible to his father.

"Just so you know, I'd never think of myself as being stuck with you." He paused with a hand on the doorknob. "Only lucky that you were by my side."

"Go! Before you make a ridiculously hormonal woman start to cry!"

He left with a wink and a wave, and the reality of the past few minutes hit like a hurricane, practically knocking Alexa off her feet. She sank into the blue love seat, the strength all but sapped from her muscles, and pulled a matching pillow against her chest.

Chance McClaren...

Seeing him had been like—seeing a ghost.

A living, breathing ghost.

Because despite that initial news report, Chance Mc-Claren had not died in the bomb attack.

Two days later, every news channel in the country was scrambling to revise their headlines. Chance was injured but alive in a hospital in some foreign city Alexa had never heard of.

But for those two days between, shock had left Alexa blessedly numb after the roller-coaster ride of emotions she'd experienced since the night they met.

She'd spent her childhood waiting for her parents to call, watching out windows for them to show up out of the blue. Waiting, wondering, hoping, only to have that hope dashed time and time again when one nanny or another would tell her that her parents weren't coming.

Until the day when her grandmother arrived and put an end to all of it. To the waiting, to the wondering, to the hoping. Her parents weren't coming. Not ever again.

She'd relived every twist and turn, every jolt and jerk, every stomach-in-her-throat loop-the-loop after Chance left, and when she read that first news report, a small, desperate part of her had been—relieved.

This child—a child she already loved, a child who would love and need her—would be all hers, and she wouldn't have to share. She wouldn't have to tell Chance he was going to be a father. Wouldn't have to worry that he would wreak havoc crashing in and out of their lives. She wouldn't have to face the pain of knowing she'd cursed her baby with a childhood destined to be so similar to her own.

She wouldn't.

Because Chance was dead.

Only then he wasn't. But it was almost easier to pretend he was.

Alexa barely had a chance to take a breath, forget to take the time she needed to recover from seeing him again, when a knock sounded at the door. She gave a small laugh as she pushed off the love seat cushions. Typical Griffin. "Forget your key?" she asked as she pulled open the door.

Only it wasn't Griffin standing on the other side. A living, breathing Chance McClaren arched a dark brow and said, "I don't recall you giving me a key...yet."

Chapter Three

Heat licked a path from her chest all the way to her cheeks, and she was tempted—seriously tempted—to slam the door in his face. But she'd been Virginia Mayhew's granddaughter too long to react in such a way. Though, really, what etiquette book had a chapter on something like this?

How to greet a weekend fling father of your unborn child. Or better yet, *What to say to a man who figuratively, if not literally, had come back from the dead.*

"Come on, Lexi, aren't you going to invite me in?"

One hand gripped the edge of the doorframe in a casual pose, but she wasn't fooled. His blue eyes were shadowed, his unshaven jaw clenched, the muscles in his arm standing out in stark relief. He looked like he'd fall over if he let go. And the heart she'd tried so hard to harden ached for him.

"Please don't call me that," she murmured even as she stepped back and allowed him into the suite and, she feared, back into her life.

She kept her back turned as she led the way toward the suite's living area. The space had felt cozy when Griffin had been there with her. Now, with Chance, she felt the walls closing in.

"What should I call you? After all, that is how you introduced yourself that night, isn't it?"

Alexa nearly groaned at the reminder. She'd been calling herself a fool ever since. What had she been thinking? One look into Chance's startling blue eyes back in the lobby, and she'd remembered. Even now a rush of energy, awareness, attraction arced between them, and Alexa knew she hadn't been thinking much at all.

For one weekend, with this one man, she'd let herself feel. She'd known there would be a price to pay for abandoning the tight control that had shaped her life for the past twenty-plus years. She just hadn't realized until she found out she was pregnant that her child would be the one to pay it. But only if she told Chance the truth...

"What do you want, Chance?" She picked up the pillow that had fallen from the love seat and carefully tucked it back against the armrest, smoothing a ruffled corner as if nothing mattered more.

"Oh, I don't know." His eyes glowed like superheated flame as she straightened to meet his gaze. "I hear congratulations are in order."

So she was right, Alexa thought. She had wounded some sense of macho pride when she pretended not to know him. Throw in an almost-engagement, and the man she'd last spoken to months ago was suddenly at her door.

She took a step backward, needing some space from the heat coming off his body in waves, only to bump up against the white wicker coffee table. He countered her move, trapping her there unless she wanted to start scrambling over furniture to try to get away. "Chance—"

"For someone who claims not to take risks, you sure move fast when you want to."

Alexa wasn't sure her skin could get much hotter without setting her hair on fire. He knew just how fast she had moved, falling into bed with him the very night they met. Looking back, the entire weekend seemed like some kind of dream, a magical moment out of time. One that, even with the pregnancy, she hadn't been able to bring herself to regret—until now. Until Chance made her feel ashamed. "I—"

"Four months, and now you're suddenly engaged?"

"Engaged? You mean Griffin?"

He raised an eyebrow. "Do you have another fiancé I don't know about?"

"No, of course not." She didn't even have the one he did know about. Not really.

"Unless…" His gaze narrowed dangerously. "Were you engaged when we met?"

"What? No! I certainly wouldn't have slept with you," she hissed beneath her breath as if the entire hotel might have been listening in, "if I'd been engaged to another man at the time."

He searched her expression, his stance easing ever so slightly at what he saw there. She caught a hint of the ocean mixed with his own masculine scent, and her focus drifted toward his lips even as she wondered if she would taste the salt on his skin…

He's here. I can't believe he's really here.

Sucking in a quick breath, Alexa snapped herself out of the dangerous direction her thoughts had taken. Chance might have just come from a walk on the beach, but she was the one who needed to throw herself into the frigid waves!

What had he been saying? Oh, right. He'd just accused

her of cheating on her fiancé. "Griffin James and I have known each other since we were children, but he only recently asked me to marry him."

"Just like that?"

"What?"

"You've known each other for years and then what? You woke up one day and decided to get married?"

"We're well suited." Alexa cringed, hearing her grandmother's words coming out of her mouth. Her grandmother would be thrilled if she accepted Griffin's proposal. Virginia had been pushing the two of them together since high school.

"Right. Whereas you and I were only well suited in bed."

Alexa stared at him. "What are you doing here, Chance?"

He opened his mouth but no sound escaped. He ran a hand through his disheveled hair, looking at a loss, out of sorts and so completely different from the man she'd met four months ago. "Hell if I know," he finally sighed.

Alexa fought it, she really did, but her heart cried out at the unexpected vulnerability in his expression. He looked…awful. At the charity auction, he'd fit in with the sophisticated crowd—breathtaking in a tuxedo that outlined his six-foot-something frame with a perfection that would bring any red-blooded woman to her knees. His dark hair had been brushed back from his wide forehead, revealing his classic bone structure, gorgeous blue eyes and a pair of dimples to die for.

Today his hair fell across that forehead in disarray. His face looked gaunt. The spark was missing from those sapphire blues, the dimples nowhere to be seen beneath the rough stubble.

Four months wasn't much time, but so much had happened. She had a new life growing inside her, and

Chance—Chance had almost died. "I heard the news reports."

Cringing, he asked, "Which one?"

"The one that said you'd been killed in a suicide bomb attack."

"Bad reporting."

"It doesn't look that far off." She hadn't noticed earlier, but he stood off-center, resting the majority of his weight on his left side. How close had he come to dying?

"I'm fine. I'll be back in the field in no time."

Right, Alexa thought bitterly, because who would let nearly getting blown up make them rethink their life choices?

A few years before her parents were killed in an avalanche while skiing in the Italian Alps, they had survived a plane crash. The small jet had experienced engine failure, and the pilot had made a miracle landing on a middle of nowhere country road. But instead of making her parents rethink their high-flying, jet-setting lifestyle, surviving the near-death incident had only made them feel that much more invincible.

Alexa could only imagine Chance would react the same—taking more risks, accepting more challenges until his luck ran out way too soon.

At the moment, though, it was hard to think about him being thousands of miles away, putting his life in danger, when he was right there, close enough to touch. And it was all Alexa could do not to erase the mere inches between them, to throw her arms around him, to see, smell, touch, *taste* that he was really and truly alive and well—

Hormones, she thought desperately. She'd read how pregnancy could lead to a skyrocketing of emotions, but the rationale failed to erase the dizzying rush of desire flooding her veins. *Nothing more than a momentary lapse.*

Unfortunately, her lapses were all too common at least

where Chance McClaren was concerned. But just because she'd made a mistake didn't mean she would keep making them. From now on, she would make no more impulsive decisions; she would do her thinking with her head, not her heart.

And certainly not with her hormones.

Taking a sanity-saving step back from the hold Chance had over her, she whispered, "You should go before…"

His lips twisted in a mockery of a smile as he came to his own conclusion as to what she was afraid might happen. "Right. Wouldn't want your fiancé catching you alone in a hotel room with a guy you slept with."

Alexa opened her mouth to argue only to stop. What would be the point? Maybe it was better for Chance to think she and Griffin were engaged.

"But don't worry. We'll have plenty of time to see each other around."

She shivered slightly at the promise—*warning*—in his expression. "Why is that?"

"Didn't my sister tell you? I'm your wedding photographer."

Alexa smiled at the waitress who topped off her glass of water before looking across the small table to find Griffin staring at her. "What?"

"You're not eating."

After the confrontation with Chance, Alexa had wanted nothing more than to escape the hotel. When Griffin returned to their suite and suggested a trip into town, she'd instantly agreed. They'd spent the afternoon browsing through the charming stores along Main Street. She would normally have loved taking in the Victorian architecture—the turrets, the wraparound porches, the elegantly detailed trim work and bright colors of the painted ladies—but she couldn't concentrate.

She sighed as she picked through her salad. Couldn't eat.

After surviving bouts of morning sickness her first trimester, her appetite had come back with a vengeance. So much so that when she'd reminded Griffin she was eating for two, he'd asked, "Are they both linebackers in the NFL?"

But now, with her nerves so frazzled from the confrontation with Chance, she could barely swallow a bite. "If you want, we can go somewhere else," Griffin offered.

He'd spotted the old-fashioned diner with its black-and-white floors, stainless-steel eat-in counter and red-vinyl-covered booths. Despite—or perhaps because of—the five-star restaurants boasted by many of his family's hotels, he'd always enjoyed a basic burger and fries.

They were seated toward the back of the diner, and Alexa had a view of the entire place. The booths and barstools were crowded with a mix of tourists and locals. Pink-uniformed waitresses called out orders to a cook behind the counter, and fifties music bounced through the speakers. The smell of grilled meat and fried food would have been mouthwatering if she'd had any kind of appetite.

"No, this is fine." She stabbed at a piece of chicken in her Cobb salad.

Dunking a fry in a pool of ketchup on the corner of his plate, Griffin casually asked, "That was him, wasn't it?"

Alexa froze, midchew, convinced he couldn't be asking what she thought he was asking. But his gaze was so certain, reminding her that she'd never been able to pull anything over on him. Still, she swallowed and reached for her glass.

"I'm sorry…" After taking a sip of slightly tart apple juice, she asked, "Who's 'him'?" Childish of her to play dumb when Griffin knew her so well. She might as well close her eyes and pretend the world—pretend *Chance McClaren*—couldn't see her.

"You know." He nodded to the spot hidden beneath the opposite end of the table. "Your baby daddy."

Alexa set her glass back on the white-fleck Formica table with a thunk. "Have I told you how much I loathe that term?"

"Do you have a better expression in mind?"

Weekend fling...

Sperm donor...

Father of her child...

None of them did anything to settle the nerves spiraling through her stomach.

"Besides, it doesn't matter what I call him. I'm still right, aren't I? He's the one."

The one. Somehow that sounded even worse than all the others. Yes, Chance McClaren was the one man who'd made her forget herself for a long weekend. The one man who'd gotten her to take a chance, to risk stepping outside her comfort zone. The one man who'd made her feel free.

A flutter of movement in her belly seemed to mock that thinking. *Not so free now.*

But Chance was not the one when it came to the man Alexa might have picked to father her child. Not the one when it came to a man she would choose for a stable, long-term relationship.

She knew that in her head, in her heart. So why didn't her stupid body get with the program and settle down? Why were chills still racing down her spine and gooseflesh rising along her skin after seeing him again?

"How did you figure it out?" Alexa had told Griffin she was pregnant, keeping most of the details, including Chance's name, to herself. She wasn't sure why, other than saying his name would have brought back even more memories. And she'd been trying so hard to forget.

"Other than the sparks you two were striking off each other?" Griffin downed a fourth of his cheeseburger with one bite before adding, "After seeing the way you reacted, I did some quick online research on the guy. Turns out he was at that benefit in Santa Barbara, the same one where you met your mystery man."

Alexa sighed, knowing Griffin had her cornered. "I still can't believe he's here. A part of me thought I'd never see him again."

"Because you thought he'd been killed?" A hint of chiding filled Griffin's voice that she hadn't told him the whole story.

"You read the reports?"

"It was hard not to. Plug McClaren's name into a search engine, and every headline touts how the guy came back from the dead."

Alexa pushed the chopped tomatoes in her salad into a small pile. "I know. And I would have told you, but you were in the middle of those meetings with your father." Meetings over Griffin's trust and the stipulations that, so far, had kept him from obtaining the money. "And by the time you were home…"

"Chance was alive."

"Yes."

"Safe to say the two of you aren't as finished as you made it seem."

Alexa shook her head. "You're wrong. It's over." She gave a half laugh. "It never really started. It was a weekend fling. Nothing more."

"You don't have weekend flings, Alexa."

"I know!" She longed to cover her face with her hands at what had been such an out-of-character thing for her to do. She feared it wasn't so out of character for Chance, yet another reason why things could never work out between them.

"So don't you think that means something?"

"That I've become a desperate, lonely woman?"

"Okay, first, that's not true. And second, there had to be something about Chance McClaren for you to sleep with him that first night." His expression was wry as he pointed out, "I've seen you take longer before deciding on a pair of shoes."

She refused to meet his gaze as she added a dash of pepper before spearing a quarter slice of hard-boiled egg. "Shoes are important."

"Allie. Come on."

Alexa swallowed. "It wouldn't work between the two of us. We're too different. We want such polar opposite things out of life. I told him that when he called. And that was before I even knew I was pregnant!"

"Wait." Griffin pointed a thick-cut fry in accusation. "You didn't tell me that."

"What?"

"That he called…or that you were the one to call things off."

"I didn't. Not really." Leaning forward, she stressed, "I hadn't heard from him in five weeks, Griffin."

"And what was Chance doing during those five weeks?"

"He—" Alexa cut herself off, realizing she hadn't asked where Chance had been or what he'd been doing. "He was probably off in some desert or jungle or swamp, God knows where."

"Which probably made it hard to make contact," Griffin chimed in with a logic that had Alexa feeling very illogical.

"Whose side are you on, anyway?"

"Yours. Always." He leaned back in the booth before saying, "I found something else when I was looking around online. Something I should have remembered. It was the twenty-year anniversary of your parents' deaths, wasn't it? Not long after you and Chance met?"

The exact anniversary had been the very day he'd called. "I don't see what that has to do with anything."

"Oh, come on, Allie. You can't tell me you don't see the similarities. But whatever your parents' faults were, they were their own. Don't hold Chance responsible for them."

"What are you saying, Griffin?"

"What you already know. He has a right to know that he's going to be a father."

The last thing Chance wanted to do that evening was head into Clearville for dinner. The Victorian town held a certain appeal for visitors and for locals who made their money off those tourists, but the place had always struck Chance as too cute. And now, as smiling pumpkins and pilgrims battled with Santa and Rudolph for prime window display real estate, it was worse than he remembered.

Rory, of course, loved it.

"I can't wait to start decorating Hillcrest for Christmas!" Wearing a thigh-length red coat, his sister already looked in the holiday spirit. She waved a hand at the glowing storefronts along Main Street. "I wanted to start putting up a few small touches here and there—just a wreath or two—but Evie insisted we wait until after Thanksgiving."

"For once, Evie and I agree," he said wryly.

"I'm so glad you'll be here for the holidays. I don't remember the last time we were all together at Christmas."

Home for the holidays? Oh, hell, no. Christmas was several weeks away, which might as well be an eternity. He wouldn't still be in Clearville then. He *couldn't* be. But even as he opened his mouth to argue, he swallowed a curse as the toe of his shoe caught on an uneven spot on the sidewalk, and his full weight landed on his right leg.

Six months, his doctors and therapists had warned him, before he could expect full range of motion. Before he could walk without limping, without pain.

"Chance—"

"I'm fine." He cut Rory off before she could ask the question he was already so sick of hearing.

"Are you sure you should be off your crutches so soon?" she pressed.

Pushing yourself won't make your body heal any faster, his doctor had warned. *You aren't building up muscle. You're regrowing bone, and that takes time.*

Chance didn't have time. He'd been riding a wave of success with recent recognition from the World Press along with nominations for international photography awards. While on the sidelines, several key assignments had been given to other photographers. He had to keep his name and his pictures out there. Whatever it took.

As they stepped inside Rolly's diner, Chance came face-to-face with another reason why he needed to get out of there. Anywhere but Clearville.

"Oh, look, there's Alexa and Griffin!" Rory announced as she sent the couple a quick wave.

Seated at a booth toward the back of the restaurant, Alexa lifted a weak hand in response while her golden boy fiancé was all smiles. As Chance's gaze caught Alexa's, as the distance between them—the crowded tables, the chattering waitresses, as the whole damn diner—disappeared in that powerful moment of memory, of connection, he could almost feel sorry for the poor SOB.

If Griffin James hadn't been the one seated across from Alexa. If he hadn't been the one holding her hand, hearing her voice, smelling the honey-lilac scent of her skin.

Sharing her hotel room...

Yeah, who was the poor SOB now?

"I didn't expect to see them here," Rory was saying as she slid into an empty booth.

Chance had had plenty of time to curse the limitations of his injury but rarely more so than in that moment. Unable to fully bend his knee, he had to take the seat on his left, to keep his right leg stretched out. A seat that faced the back of the restaurant and gave him a perfect view of Alexa and her fiancé.

"Yeah, this is hardly Alexa's kind of place."

Rory frowned as she lifted the laminated menu that probably hadn't changed since the last time Chance had eaten there. "How would you know?"

"I know...women like her," he finished. "Wealthy, spoiled, too good for everyone around her."

Not that Alexa had seemed like any of those things the night they met.

Setting the menu aside, his sister took a deep breath. "You know how much I hate admitting Evie's right, but you really do need to get on board if you're going to be our photographer."

If? *If?* She'd all but begged him to fill in! "I told you I'd get a haircut and all that."

"I'm not talking about how you look. I'm talking about your attitude about love and marriage...and women."

"Excuse me?"

"I know Lisette did a number on you—"

Now it was his turn to toss the menu aside. "This has nothing to do with Lisette," he stated flatly.

"Then what?"

"It's—"

We come from different worlds, Chance.

He watched as Griffin James, a man very much a part of Alexa's world, reached over and cupped her cheek in his palm.

"Nothing," he told Rory finally. "It's nothing."

Chapter Four

"Don't worry. Everything's under control." Even as Alexa spoke the words into her cell phone, she fought a burst of hysterical laughter that would certainly be enough to send her grandmother's panicked assistant over the edge. Not to mention the state it would leave Alexa in.

Under control? As she listened to Raquel rattle off the dozens of details her grandmother had needed handled in the three days since Alexa left, she couldn't imagine anything being further from the truth.

Chance was alive.

Chance was here.

She needed to tell Chance he was the father of her baby.

The phrases had circled endlessly through her mind, robbing her of any hope of a good night's sleep. She'd always been an early riser, part of the strict schedule her grandmother had established and one Alexa couldn't seem to break no matter how hard she tried. Or no matter how many hours she'd spent tossing and turning the night before.

Her doctor had encouraged exercise and warned her about too much stress, so Alexa had set out on a early morning walk. As she'd breathed in the cool morning fog, a bit of pressure eased from her chest. The breeze rustled through the pines, carrying a hint of salt air, and she was glad she'd thought to grab a thigh-length beige sweater to wear over her tunic-style cream blouse and tan leggings.

But any sense of relaxation had come to an abrupt end as she remembered that Chance wasn't the only one Alexa needed to tell about her pregnancy. And while she had no idea how Chance was going to react, she had a good idea what her proper, old-fashioned grandmother would have to say.

Tuning back into the conversation and Raquel's laundry list of concerns, she reassured the younger woman, "You'll do fine."

"But the Giving Thanks benefit—"

"Everything is going as scheduled. I confirmed with the vendors this morning." Alexa could hear Raquel relaying the information back to her grandmother and Virginia's protests in the background. "Tell my grandmother—"

"You can tell me yourself, Alexa." Virginia Mayhew's crisp voice cut across the line.

"Like I was saying to Raquel, everything is under control. I contacted—"

"*You* should be here working on the benefit. How does it look for you to be off on vacation at the most critical time of the fund-raising season?"

Considering she typically dealt with vendors by phone or email, Alexa knew things didn't "look" any different. She also knew that wasn't her grandmother's point. Alexa was the face of the foundation, and that face was always supposed to be in the public eye.

But Alexa was tired of constantly living behind a public persona. She wanted to live her own life. A life where she could go outside without the perfect clothes, perfect hair, perfect makeup. A life where *she* could be something less than perfect. "It's only for a few days, Grandmother."

"This isn't a good time. I told you that before you left."

"Yes, you did," Alexa acknowledged, but it was never a good time. Which was why she hadn't taken a vacation in...she couldn't even remember how long. "I'll be home soon."

Alexa hung up feeling the familiar weight of expectation pressing on her chest. She had started volunteering for the Mayhew Foundation when she was still in her teens and had dedicated her adult life to helping raise money for those in need.

Taking a deep breath, Alexa pressed the button on the side of her phone. For the first time, she was going to think of *her* needs. She'd longed for a break from the nonstop schedule for the past year or so, but doubted she would have made the stand if not for her pregnancy.

Growing up in her grandmother's house, Alexa's world had been filled with directives as to what a Mayhew did not do. A Mayhew did not slouch, did not sulk, did not argue, did not cry...

Only with Griffin had Alexa ever felt she could let down the walls her grandmother's rules had built around her and truly be herself. Only with Griffin...and with Chance.

Not that her feelings for the two men were at all the same. With Griffin, she felt safe. With him, she could say and do whatever she wanted.

With Chance, she felt *dangerous*. With him, she had said and done things she'd never imagined, and now...

Alexa was certain getting pregnant following a weekend fling would fall within the "did not" constraints.

But telling her grandmother would have to wait. First, she needed to tell Chance.

Some wistful part of her hoped that he would be stunned, yet overjoyed by the news. Sweeping her up into his arms the same way he'd swept her off her feet in Santa Barbara.

After confessing she'd never done something so out of character, so impetuous as to sleep with a man she'd just met, they'd teasingly come up with the list of crazy, adrenaline-fueled exploits for her to try next—all with Chance right by her side.

How about rushing headlong into the adventures of parenthood, Chance? How do you feel about holding my hand on that wild ride?

But after seeing him again, it was almost impossible to imagine a happily-ever-after ending. The charmingly seductive man she'd met the night of the charity ball seemed so...different now. Had the injury somehow changed him? Or had she allowed herself to start to fall for a man who didn't even exist?

Maybe he would even deny the baby was his. She supposed that would serve her right after foolishly pretending not to know him, and after she'd told him not to contact her in the first place, but the idea of Chance turning his back on their child made her heart ache.

I want this baby. A child to care for, to nurture, to love. The baby might have been unexpected, but not unwanted. Never unwanted. At least not by her.

Alexa slid the phone into the pocket of her sweater and glanced back toward the hotel. She'd walked farther than she'd realized, the Victorian turrets silhouetted by the gray autumn sky. She thought she'd taken the path that would lead to the gazebo Rory mentioned during their tour, but instead she caught a glimpse of a small cottage between the trees. She couldn't help smiling as she recalled Griffin's comment. If Rory was Snow White, then Alexa could certainly imagine seven dwarves living in the cute stone and wood structure.

She was tempted to take a closer look but stopped short when the front door opened. Her breath caught in her throat as Chance stepped outside, erasing any thoughts of fantasy dwarves and replacing them instead with the reality of six feet of living, breathing male.

Standing on the small porch, he stretched his neck from one side to the other. As his gaze swung in her direction, Alexa automatically ducked. She cringed, imagining what her grandmother would say if she could see her now, crouching behind a row of hedges before he could spot her.

A Mayhew does not skulk in the bushes, Alexa.

As she watched from her leafy vantage point, he ran both hands through his tousled dark hair and arched his back. Her mouth went dry as his faded T-shirt rode up above the loose waistband of his sweatpants, revealing a slice of muscled abs and tanned skin. Heat licked at her cheeks, and she wasn't sure which flame burned brighter—her arousal or her embarrassment.

Hiding was one thing. Spying was something else entirely!

Really, she needed to stop. And she would…in a minute.

Because beyond arousal and embarrassment, Alexa couldn't help noticing that his sweatpants weren't just loose. The elastic band threatened to slip past his hip bones.

Her stomach clutched. How much weight had he lost? As he took a few steps, his limp was more noticeable than the day before. Was his leg worse…or with no one around and no reason to pretend everything was all right, was he allowing himself to give in to the pain?

He would hate for her to witness even a momentary weakness, and she carefully ducked deeper into her hiding spot. She'd wait a moment or two for Chance to go inside before making her way back to the hotel.

She hazarded another glance toward the cottage and breathed a sigh of relief when she saw the porch was empty. She needed to tell Chance about the baby, but not yet. Not until she could be calm and in control, and until she was sure she could do that… Well, she'd be hiding in the bushes.

Pushing to her feet, she swore beneath her breath as the branches caught in the loose knit of her sweater. She nearly jumped out of her skin when a deep voice behind her asked, "You lose something?"

She spun around, slipping on the damp ground and stumbling against the solid, masculine wall of his chest. Chance instinctively caught her, his hands warm and roughly seductive against her upper arms. Each individual fingertip struck a pinpoint of sensation, and the back of his thumbs pressed against her overly sensitive breasts.

She jumped back quickly, but the damage had already been done. Her body still tingled from the sudden contact, the air around them still crackled with undeniable intensity, and she knew she'd made a big mistake not leaving when she'd had the chance.

"You scared me half to death!"

He gave her a sardonic grin. "Sorry, didn't mean to sneak up on you while you were…?"

His words drifted away, a dark brow winged upward in query, and Alexa wrapped her sweater around her waist. "I was out for a walk," she sniffed, trying to maintain an air of dignity.

His smirk marked her as a liar. "Next time maybe you'll try the beach. That's my favorite spot."

Alexa had a view of the rugged coastline from her suite along with the uneven, rocky pathway that led to the beach. It was not what she'd consider a leisurely stroll. As he turned, Alexa realized he hadn't been stretching on the porch; he'd been warming up.

Without stopping to think, she reached out and caught his arm. His skin was warm, undeniably masculine muscle beneath a dusting of dark hair, and for a moment, she forgot what it was she wanted to say.

Forgot everything but the memory of sliding her hand down that same arm as she'd slipped the white tuxedo shirt from his broad shoulders.

Chance froze beneath her touch, and Alexa swallowed. "Are—are you sure that's a good idea?"

His heated gaze dropped to where her hand still rested on his forearm. "Are you sure *that's* a good idea?"

Snatching her hand back, she said, "I meant pushing yourself so hard."

"Hard was being stuck in traction. You don't have to worry about me, Alexa. I heal fast."

She couldn't imagine what that had been like for him. For a man who was always on the move to not just be stuck in a hospital bed, but to be held in place, immobilized by ropes and pulleys.

She was dying to ask him what had happened, what he'd gone through, beyond the news reports she could barely bring herself to read. After that first devastating headline, she hadn't known what to believe. Was he truly recovering or was that information wrong, as well?

But she knew better than to expect an honest answer. Especially not after he pinned her with a look and added, "Before long, I'll move on like nothing ever happened."

The way he thought she'd moved on to Griffin? Alexa swallowed but asked, "What about your job here?"

"You mean…wedding photographer? That *isn't* my job, Alexa. That's a favor to my sister. One I never should have agreed to," he added beneath his breath.

"Why? Photographing weddings will be a piece of cake compared to what you're used to."

"What I'm used to—" he muttered. "What I'm used to is photographing some of the worst of humanity. I'm not sure I trust myself to still recognize the good."

His vulnerability grabbed hold of the secret she kept, tugging the words straight from her heart. She longed to reassure him of the good in the world, of the something *great* the two of them had created together. But would he see their baby that way? When he was so dead set on pushing himself to get better so that he could *move on*?

So instead, she pointed out, "Your sister clearly trusts you."

"My sister tends to trust everyone. It's one of her biggest failings." Chance glanced around the towering trees and the Victorian hotel in the distance. "Rory's always thought this place was magic."

With her arms still crossed at her waist, Alexa could feel the slight swell of her belly. She and Chance had made a baby. It might not have been magic, but as far as Alexa was concerned, it was a tiny miracle.

A miracle she needed to share. Swallowing against the lump in her throat, she whispered, "Chance…"

He straightened abruptly. "You should go. I'm sure your fiancé is wondering where you are."

"Chance, we need to talk—"

"I think you said everything you needed to say during our last phone call."

Goodbye was pretty much all they'd said during that phone call, and so much had happened since then. Finding out that she was pregnant, the bombing, the reports of his death. "But…"

He started to turn away, then stopped. Alexa's heart jumped to her throat as he reached up a hand and brushed his fingers through her hair. A muscle in his jaw clenched, and she could only stare helplessly into the firestorm of emotions in his sapphire eyes.

For a split second, she thought he was going to pull her closer, to kiss her the way he had that first night underneath the sparkling stars. To kiss her the way he had every night since in her dreams.

His voice gravel rough, he said, "I think you must have dropped this."

Only after he moved away from her did she lift a hand to the spot above her ear. Her fingers brushed against a thin piece of metal. She pulled the hairpin from her hair and stared at the bejeweled butterfly clip she hadn't seen in four months.

Not since she wore it the night of the charity event in Santa Barbara.

"Doesn't the gazebo look amazing?" Rory asked Chance, her smile almost blinding in an otherwise overcast day.

He lifted a shoulder in a shrug as he adjusted the camera to account for the hazy morning. His sister was wearing a bright red sweater over a black-and-white polka-dot dress—an outfit that was sure to pop against the white lattice of the gazebo.

He cringed at the thought, left over from his days of fashion photography where he'd worked behind a camera to capture fantasy rather than reality. He would have thought after seeing behind the curtain, knowing all the hours of hair and makeup and wardrobe that went into creating a picture-perfect shot, that he would have been able to tell the difference.

And yet for months, Lisette had had him completely fooled.

He had to give her credit for one thing, though. The first time they met she'd told him she would do anything to make it as a fashion model. She'd been up-front about that. He just hadn't realized "anything" included lying, manipulating and finally cheating on him.

When he confronted her, she'd pleaded, she'd cried, she'd begged him not to throw away everything they had over a "mistake." But in that moment, he finally realized he'd witnessed that full range of emotions from behind the camera and that it was all a performance. When he refused to budge, Lisette had dropped the act.

We're not so different, Chance, so don't pretend you're better than me. We both know our careers are more important than anything...or anyone.

Chance wasn't so sure that was true ten years ago, but it was now.

His hands tightened on his camera as he thought of the call from his editor the other day. "I'm sorry, Chance," the man had added after telling him he was giving the prime assignment to another photojournalist. "You know we can't sit on breaking stories. If there was any way to know when you'll be back…"

Chance had swallowed the promises he longed to make. As much as he wanted to grab his gear and go, he couldn't. The harder he pushed his body, the harder his body was pushing back.

Are you sure that's a good idea?

He'd barely been able to get out of bed after the grueling pace he'd set that day on the beach. He couldn't even pretend work had been the only thing on his mind as he'd pounded across the hard-packed sand until his lungs were burning and his leg was on fire.

Because hadn't he wanted to believe he'd seen something in Alexa's eyes when he'd run into her outside the cottage? Something that said what they'd shared had been more than a final fling before marrying her "well-suited" fiancé?

Chance swore. Maybe that old expression was true—once a fool, always a fool.

"Sorry, Chance, what was that?" Rory asked, breaking into his thoughts and returning his focus to where it should have been all along.

"I was just thinking…" He waved a hand at the gazebo with its lattice trim and elegant scrollwork. "Looks the same as it always did."

"Right, the same as it did ten or fifteen years ago when you last saw it. You weren't here a few months ago when it was practically falling down." Her smile turned almost secretive as she ran a hand over the railing leading to the circular platform. "Jamison did an amazing job remodeling it in time for his best friend's wedding. This place is…special to us."

Special? Combine that with the satisfied look on his sister's face and—Chance groaned. "Okay, stop. Now! Before I have to scrub my brain out with soap."

"Oh, grow up! We're both adults here."

"Uh, no. I'm an adult and you're my baby sister, and if you tell me much more than you already have, I'll have to punch your lawyer-boy fiancé in the face. Where is he, anyway?"

His sister had asked him to take some pictures for updating the hotel's website and for new brochures touting the place as *the* wedding spot. Rory and Jamison were going to pose as a happy couple with the gazebo as a romantic backdrop, but his sister's fiancé had yet to show. "Didn't you say you had a deadline to get these shots to the printer?"

Rory sighed. "I do, but Jamison decided to stay in San Francisco for another day or two. His former in-laws are having a hard time with Hannah moving away."

Chance didn't feel much sympathy for the older couple, knowing the problems they'd caused when Rory and Jamison first got together. "So they call, and he automatically runs home?"

"Like I said, they're having a hard time. Jamison is doing all he can to make the transition easier." Rory lifted her chin to a stubborn—and familiar—angle.

Chance knew she wouldn't say anything against her fiancé, but he had to wonder. "Are you sure Jamison isn't simply making it easier for his in-laws to manipulate him? And letting them use his daughter to do it?"

"They've lost their daughter, and Hannah is their only grandchild. This isn't *easy* on anyone. And besides, they're her family."

"Family," he echoed. "You say that as if it makes everything and anything okay. Even if—"

We just want what's best for you, Chance.

Even if they didn't know him at all.

"Chance…"

His sister was no fool. But whatever Rory suspected, he wasn't going there. Not now. Probably not ever when for all he knew, Rory felt the same way.

Maybe—maybe it would be better if his leg never healed…

"So if Jamison's a no-show, what are we doing here? You want some shots just of the gazebo?"

Lingering worry and hurt swirled in his sister's gaze. "No, I—" Her expression cleared, and she glanced over his shoulder. "Oh, perfect. Here they are now! When Jamison had to leave town, I asked another couple to step in."

Chance knew without looking back exactly who was standing behind him. The hair on the back of his neck rose as a familiar awareness surged through him. He didn't need to turn around, but like some kind of polarized magnet, he couldn't stop the sudden pull.

As Alexa's startled gaze locked on his, Chance's hands tightened around the camera. He was sure heiress and philanthropist Alexa Mayhew had never given modeling a second's thought, but she could have made a fortune at it. Wearing a soft pink sweater draped over a loose floral print dress, she looked as fashionable as ever. Her blond hair fell to her shoulders in soft waves, tucked back behind one ear.

It was all Chance could do to keep from lifting his camera and snapping the moment.

In the months since that weekend in Santa Barbara, especially those first agonizing weeks in the hospital, he'd regretted not taking Alexa's picture when he'd had the chance.

Oh, with her family's wealth and Alexa's status as the face of her grandmother's foundation, he could have found dozens of images online. But none that he had taken. He wanted to photograph the Alexa only he could see, the sensual side she'd revealed to him during their weekend together. He wanted to capture that part of her for himself—

And didn't that sound downright creepy?

"I asked Griffin and Alexa to help out, and they agreed," Rory was saying behind him.

Because yes, Alexa's fiancé was there, too, but Chance couldn't drag his gaze away from Alexa.

Ever since the morning outside the cottage two days

ago, Chance had done his damnedest to keep his distance, but the hotel simply wasn't big enough for both of them. There were still those unavoidable moments. A brief second when they passed each other in the lobby. When they'd seen each other across the hotel restaurant. And he'd felt it every damn time.

The rush, the attraction, the awareness arcing between them. As powerful and elemental as a bolt of lightning, raising the hair on his arms on end and making him feel... alive.

And as she drew closer, a flash of gold and diamond in her hair sparkled despite the cloudy skies. Her chin lifted, almost as if she were challenging him to notice, to remember...

Chance swore beneath his breath. Like he needed the reminder. Hell, he'd given the damn thing back to her as a way to cut ties. To convince his stupid heart of what he hadn't been able to bring himself to believe—it was over.

She'd been more than clear in that last phone call, so why would she choose to wear the hairpin now?

During his months together with Lisette, he hadn't figured her out until it was too late and the damage to his career had already been done. And in hindsight, without head-over-heels lust blinding him, the attention-grabbing, spoiled beauty wasn't that hard to pin down.

But did he really think he'd have a clue what was going through the mind of a far more complicated woman like Alexa after their single weekend together?

Color rising in her cheeks, she finally broke the lingering glance and turned to her fiancé. "What did we agree to?" she asked quietly.

"You didn't tell her?" Rory asked.

Griffin was all smiles as he shot Alexa a wink that had

Chance's hands tightening on his camera. "I thought it would be a surprise. Surprise!"

Rory laughed and explained, "We need some pictures taken for our website and for some brochures for the hotel. We're in a bit of a time crunch and... Anyway, I need a couple to pose with the gazebo as the romantic backdrop, and when my fiancé got called away, I thought you and Griffin would be perfect! If you don't mind, Alexa?"

Griffin was already guiding her toward the gazebo's steps, his arm wrapped possessively around her slender waist. "You're always willing to help out when someone needs a hand."

Chance could see she was practically dragging her feet across the damp ground. "Of course, I'd like to help but—"

"It will only be a few shots. And Chance is a marvelous photographer."

Alexa drew in a deep breath and offered Rory a smile. "Just a few shots," she agreed.

"Perfect!" His sister clapped her hands in excitement. "Chance, are you ready?"

Ready to see Alexa in the arms of another man? Because walking in on Lisette hadn't been bad enough?

Clearly the universe felt he hadn't learned his lesson when it came to falling for the wrong woman.

Chapter Five

As the face of her grandmother's charity, Alexa had learned long ago to hide behind a smile. Band canceled at the last minute? No problem. Famous couple who were presenting the charity with a check were now at war? Piece of cake. Countless minor emergencies filling her days, her nights, her weekends, her life? That's what she was there for.

But this…

"If you could see your boyfriend's face right about now…" Griffin said in a low voice as they posed on the gazebo with Chance as the photographer and Rory as artistic director. "He looks like he wants to kill me."

"*I* want to kill you right now!" Pins and needles pricked every inch of her flesh, heightening her awareness to the point when every breath seemed an effort and she could count every single beat of her heart. Suffocating beneath Chance's impassive stare, she wanted to sink through the gazebo floor. "And he's not my boyfriend."

Self-consciously, she lifted her hand to tuck her hair behind her ear only to remember her hair was already back. Held in place by the butterfly hairpin Chance had returned to her two days ago.

She hadn't known exactly when she'd lost the hairpin the night of the charity event. Down in the marble and gold lobby as she mingled with the other arriving guests? In the ballroom during the five-course meal? On the dance floor where Chance first held her in his arms? Or later when he'd held her in her hotel room?

The impact of Chance returning the hairpin hadn't immediately struck her. She'd left it behind; he'd found it and returned it. Except he couldn't have possibly known he would see her. Not at Hillcrest House. Possibly never again, considering the way they'd left things with that last phone call.

So why, when fate...or *whatever* brought them back together again all these months later, had he still been carrying her hairpin with him?

You don't have weekend flings, Alexa, Griffin had pointed out. *Don't you think that means something?*

She was still coming to grips with what that weekend meant to her. It was easier to believe Chance had walked away without looking back. But what if some part of him wanted to hold on to what they'd found that weekend—like he'd held on to that hairpin? What if he'd wanted to *stay*?

"You'll forgive me. You always do." Griffin's expression turned serious as he added, "It's been three days, Allie. You said you were going to tell him."

"No, you said I *should.*"

"And deep down you agree whether you're willing to admit it or not. You just need a little push."

And Griffin was good at pushing her. Into the deep end of the pool when she'd been nine and too scared to jump despite months of private swimming lessons. Out from behind a curtain and onto center stage at one of the first fund-raising events she'd organized.

And now he was pushing her to talk to Chance.

"Griffin—"

"Just a second." Stepping back, he reached into his pocket and pulled out his phone. After a quick look at the screen, he shot her a sympathetic glance. "Sorry, I've got to take this. I'll just be a minute."

Reaching out, Alexa desperately grabbed his arm. "Griffin!"

Leaning close, he pressed a kiss against her temple. "Talk to him," he murmured before he backed down the stairs and walked away.

Standing alone in the gazebo, Alexa felt ridiculously abandoned. "I'm sure he'll be back in just a minute," she told Chance and Rory, certain of no such thing.

Five minutes later and even that small amount of certainty started to wane. But when Chance lifted the camera strapped over his head, she pleaded, "Can't we wait just a few minutes longer?" She'd promised—or at least Griffin had promised—to help Rory, and Alexa didn't want to let the other woman down. "Griffin—"

"I'm not waiting for Griffin," Chance stated flatly. "Here."

Rory's eyes widened as she fumbled with the camera her brother handed to her. "Chance, what are you doing?"

"Point and shoot, Rory. It's not that hard."

"Not that hard? Easy for you to say! If I end up breaking this thing—"

"You won't."

But instead of turning and walking away like Alexa thought he was going to, Chance stalked toward her. Reaching out, she grabbed hold of the gazebo's railing as she felt herself swaying closer as he stomped up the steps.

His gaze captured hers, and her thoughts flashed to that night four months ago.

Chance backing her into the bedroom, his low laughter striking sparks along every inch of her exposed skin when she'd suggested turning off the lights.

Do you always kiss with your eyes closed, Lexi?

Maybe, she had confessed while thinking, *Among other things.*

Then prepare to see all you've been missing, he vowed, *and to say she'd had her eyes opened was a serious understatement...*

"Your fiancé's an idiot."

"Excuse me?" Alexa blinked, the muttered words not the ones she'd thought she'd hear.

"He's an idiot to walk away from you."

Conscious of his sister only a few yards away, fiddling uncertainly with the camera in her hands, Alexa murmured, "Well, at least I can be sure Griffin's coming back."

"You made it pretty damn clear you didn't want me back, princess."

In the days that followed that magical weekend, doubts had quickly crept in. That instant connection...it couldn't have been as strong as she remembered. The feeling of belonging she'd found in his arms...that was all part of the fantasy. None of it was real because she didn't believe in love at first sight, did she...

Did she?

She couldn't. Not with a man like Chance McClaren. A man who lived life in a lane so fast it didn't have a speed limit, a man who would leave her time and time again before leaving her for the last time.

So she convinced herself the connection wasn't strong, and she had told him she didn't want to see him again.

"Um, are you sure about this, Chance?" Rory called

out, the camera that had looked so much a part of Chance held awkwardly in her much smaller hands.

"You wanted a couple to smile for the camera, right?" he called over his shoulder. "So come on, Lexi," he said beneath his breath. "Smile."

Nerves carved a hole in her stomach as she inhaled the scent of his aftershave. He'd gotten a haircut since she'd seen him last and had scraped away the thick stubble coating his rugged jaw. But for all his instructions, his unsmiling features appeared carved from granite.

"No one is going to believe we're a couple. Not even in a photograph."

Bending his head low to hers in what Alexa inanely realized would make a poignant picture, Chance murmured, "Just fake it… You know, like you did in Santa Barbara."

"Well—" Rory cleared her throat as she handed the camera back to Chance "—I think we got some…interesting shots."

Though her smile remained in place, he couldn't possibly miss the "what the heck was that?" arch to her eyebrows. He couldn't begin to explain to his sister what had just happened. Hell, he couldn't explain it to himself.

One minute he'd been photographing Alexa and Griffin, clinging to every ounce of control he possessed to keep from storming up the gazebo stairs and knocking the other man into next week, and then in the next—the guy was gone, walking off and leaving Alexa alone.

Embarrassed color kissed her cheeks in the fading light. She'd lifted a hand to her hair, and he couldn't help noticing once more that Griffin James had yet to put a ring on Alexa's slender finger. In fact, the only diamonds she wore were the ones Chance had given to her. Or at least had given back to her.

And before he could take a moment to talk himself out of it, he had climbed those steps, but the only blows had been the ones Alexa landed.

No one is going to believe we're a couple.

How many times did she need to tell him? he asked himself as he shoved his camera and lenses into his bag. He didn't belong in her world, and she'd already chosen a man who did. End of story.

So he'd shot back that jackass comment about faking it, determined to hold on to his self-righteous anger only to lose it the moment he wrapped his arms around her. Desire thrummed through his veins and it had taken all his self-control not to pull her body tight to his until he could feel every inch of her against every inch of him.

It was goodbye, he'd told himself, and this time when he walked away, there'd be no looking back. Just moving forward, the way he had always done. Onto the next job, onto the next shoot. His life was his work. In the field, he was known for his single-minded concentration. His ability to focus on the shot and block out all other distractions around him.

But Alexa was a distraction unlike any he'd ever known. With her slender arms around his neck and her honey-lilac scent haunting his senses, Chance didn't know how he was supposed to let her go.

He'd never been one for holding on, had always been the one to leave—like he had left Alexa after their weekend together. But she'd followed him. In his thoughts, in his dreams, in the darkest moments after the explosion when her presence—imagined though it was—had pulled him through.

"Chance."

"Don't," he'd protested gruffly, sure she was going to remind him once again of the differences in their lives.

He might have made a name for himself as a photo-journalist, but that didn't mean he fit in Alexa's wealthy, privileged world. So why had hearing her say the words hurt so much more than he'd expected?

"Don't say anything. Just…"

"Feel?" she'd whispered back, her voice breaking on the word and on the memory.

But that was the problem. He felt too much for a woman promised to another man. How many times had he told himself over the past months that those nights in Santa Barbara weren't as incredible as he remembered? That the long, lonely nights spent in some godforsaken war-torn country had somehow magnified his last pleasurable experience into so much more than it was?

Like putting the object of a crush on some untouchable pedestal, his memory elevated his experience with Alexa to a height real life could never equal.

But after touching her again, holding her in his arms, Chance knew it was all a lie. The reality of Alexa was more than memory, more than imagination could ever offer.

His movements were rough, impatient as he jerked the zipper on his camera bag closed. He needed to get the hell out of Clearville. He'd known coming here was a mistake, as much of one as going home had been.

He had a studio apartment in LA he saw half a dozen times a year at most. He could stay there. The three flights of stairs would be hell on his leg but a picnic compared to what staying in Clearville was doing to the rest of him.

Strains of music drifted out over the grounds, and Rory glanced back toward the hotel. "We have an anniversary party set for this evening. Sounds like the DJ is getting set up. Alexa, why don't you come with me? I'm sure you'd enjoy seeing the way we've decorated for the event."

"I'll wait here for Griffin, and we'll join you in a minute."

"Oh, okay. Um, Chance, you'll need to email the final shots over to the printer."

"I'll go through and do some touch-up work and send them over. Unless you want to have final say?"

"No, of course not. After all, you are the *professional*."

He didn't miss the slight emphasis on the last word. A reminder that Alexa was a guest and a potential Hillcrest bride…

"I can't imagine what your sister is thinking," Alexa muttered as Rory walked away.

"You're worried what my sister is thinking? I figured you'd be more concerned about your fiancé."

Her gaze cut to his, her expression a little wounded, a little guilty. "Chance, there's something I need to tell you… About Griffin…and about our time together in Santa Barbara."

"You've said enough already, and it's not like I haven't heard it all before."

"What—what does that mean?"

"Do you think you're the first rich girl to go slumming?"

Her jaw dropped. "You think— That is *not* what I was doing. If anyone is a fake, Chance McClaren, it's you! You played me in Santa Barbara. You fooled me into thinking you were charming and—and sensitive—and kind."

"I'm still plenty charming when I want to be."

He advanced on her, but she held her ground. Reminding him once again that his golden goddess had a spine of steel.

"Oh, you'd like to think so, wouldn't you? But I've got news for you. You're like the chicken pox. Now that I've had you, I'm immune."

Her head was raised to a haughty height, but that only made the pulse pounding in her long, elegant neck more noticeable. He cupped his hand around her nape, her silken hair teasing his skin as his thumb laid claim to that tell-tale throbbing. "You sure about that, princess? 'Cause I'm more than ready to put it to the test."

Alexa gasped his name when he pulled her body flush with his, but that wasn't what held Chance in place. Instead, it was the soft strains of a familiar melody—the song they had danced to in Santa Barbara.

They both froze, caught in the moment…in the memory.

Anger, desire, longing—all of it charged the air around them until the hair on the back of his neck rose. Alexa's lips parted, the slight intake of breath enough to draw him even closer, to pull him into the promise of her kiss and the memory of making love.

Until the music cut off abruptly, putting a sudden end to something that had never truly started. The empty silence was jarring, too…loud for him to ignore all he couldn't say to a woman engaged to another man.

Chance ignored the sharp pain in his leg as he jerked away. "Go back to your world, Alexa, and stay out of mine."

The past few minutes should have sent her scurrying back to her fiancé. Hell, she was right after all. He wasn't the man she'd met in Santa Barbara. He couldn't blame her for not recognizing him. At the moment, he barely recognized himself.

But instead she stood her ground, her eyes glittering with unshed tears as she raised her arms from her sides. "I can't."

"Why not?"

"Because I'm pregnant!"

Chapter Six

Blinking back furious tears, Alexa couldn't imagine a worse way to tell Chance about the baby. Shouting out the words in a fit of anger and hurt and…desire. That was as far from the calm, logical conversation she'd planned as she could get. But maybe she shouldn't even have been surprised. From the moment she met Chance McClaren, her plans had all landed in one huge handbasket.

"Pregnant?"

He echoed the word blankly, a mix of consonants and vowels that held no possible meaning in his world. "How—"

"You have to ask?"

"How do you know it's mine?"

Alexa told herself she'd expected the question, that it was her own fault Chance had to ask. But it didn't stop the hurt slicing through her. "It's yours." Still seeing the suspicion in his eyes, she said, "Griffin's a friend. Just a friend."

"A friend you were going to marry."

"He asked me to marry him. I didn't say yes."

"You sure as hell didn't say no or the two of you wouldn't be here, looking at a wedding venue." His gaze narrowed to a thin slice of blue. "He knows, doesn't he?"

"About the baby? Yes."

"You told him, but you didn't tell me." His voice had a hollow sound to it as if she'd cut the heart out of him and left him empty inside.

She forced herself to face the truth. She'd started to fall for him that weekend in Santa Barbara. She wasn't sure she believed in love at first sight, but she'd felt something. Something magical. She never would have slept with him if she hadn't. That was why she'd been so hurt when she hadn't heard from him. When the days of loving someone who would leave her without a backward glance had returned with a vengeance.

And when she found out she was pregnant…

She hadn't wanted her child to feel that same longing, that same pain.

"I needed someone to talk to, and Griffin's always been there for me…as a friend. He's always been the person I turn to, the person I count on—"

"The person you were counting on to raise my child?"

"Chance—"

"How the hell did you expect me to be there when you'd already given me the 'hit the road' speech? I wasn't there? I wasn't someone you could trust? How am I supposed to trust *you* when you were the one keeping the fact that you're pregnant a secret? You should have told me, Alexa. Me! As soon as you found out."

"You're right, Chance. This is all my fault. I really should have tried harder to get ahold of you. I should have— What? Dug out my Ouija board to let my dead baby daddy know he was going to be a father?"

Shock washed over his features, wiping away some of her anger. "I *tried* to get ahold of you, and I couldn't. The cell number you'd given me went straight to voice mail, so I reached out to the last magazine you'd published with. They wouldn't tell me anything other than that you were on assignment and then—"

Her voice broke as the memories, the pain she'd buried, denied, rose to the surface. As fresh as if she were just hearing the news. As real as if Chance was lying broken and bleeding a half a world away rather than living, breathing in front of her.

"Alexa…"

Ignoring him, she pointed a shaking finger into his chest. "So don't tell me about what I should have done."

"The reports were wrong. You know that. You must have heard that later. I'm here. I'm fine."

"This time. But next time when you aren't so lucky? When the reports are right? I know what it's like to lose my parents. I don't want to— I don't want that for our child."

"Alexa—"

Brushing the tears from her cheeks, Alexa rushed past Chance, not stopping when he called after her. Not surprised when he didn't come after her.

But at least this time she was the one to walk away.

Chance didn't know how most men reacted to finding out they were going to be a father, but as soon as the initial shock wore off, his first instinct was to run. As far and as fast as he could—which took him only a mile down the beach. The pathetically short distance and the amount of time it took to get that far only added to the trapped, suffocating feeling.

You can't outrun this one.

The mocking sound of his conscience pounded in his

head, louder than the cool ocean air rasping in and out of his lungs, louder than the waves breaking against the shoreline. A million miles wouldn't be far enough to distance himself from the panic that had set in the moment Alexa broke the news.

A father.

Bending at the waist, he braced his hands on his knees and wondered for a moment if he was going to be sick.

He was going to be a father.

He should have been excited. He should have been overjoyed. Instead, all he felt was…guilt. And fear.

Despite the risks he'd taken in life, Chance had never given much thought to dying. Not even with his list of close calls as a kid to the more recent bomb attack. Dying was inevitable regardless of how he lived his life. He could take calculated risks or he could live life in a bubble, but one way or the other, the end result was the same.

Worrying about it didn't change a thing.

But the idea that he could have died without knowing he was going to be a father, that his child could have grown up without ever knowing him, hit hard. As hard as the blow Alexa had delivered in telling him she was pregnant in the first place.

Expect the unexpected.

It was a familiar motto in the field where things rarely went as smoothly as planned on paper. He'd learned to think fast and move faster. But as he stood on the beach watching the waves rush toward the shore, the sand beneath his feet might as well have been quicksand.

He couldn't move, couldn't think.

Alexa was right. For most of his adult life, he'd avoided commitment, ties, responsibilities beyond those that came with his job. Hell, even when it came to his career, he'd made the decision to work freelance, where he was able to choose which assignment to accept and which to turn down.

He had the freedom to pack up and hit the road—just like he had that morning in Santa Barbara when he'd left Alexa behind. Sure, he'd called a few weeks later after the assignment ended and he was back in town. Thinking they could pick up where they left off. But was she really supposed to be thrilled when he called with nothing more to offer than another weekend of sex and five-star room service?

Of course she wanted more. She deserved more, and now with a baby on the way… The only question was did Chance have it within him to give more? Or was he going to leave that to Alexa's *good friend* Griffin James?

Chance wasn't sure how long he stood on the beach, but the lights in the hotel were glowing by the time he started back. Music drifted through the night air, and a flurry of activity surrounded the large tent set up on the south lawn. The white canvas gleamed thanks to the moonlit night and the hundreds of twinkle lights shining like stars in the nearby trees. Staff members were scrambling around, calling out instructions to each other as they put on the final touches for the anniversary party. Place settings, water glasses and a red rose on every table.

Rory did an amazing job, but his sister was the last person he wanted to run into. Sucking in a deep breath, he turned away. The loose gravel path crunched beneath his uneven gait, but he pushed forward. If he could just keep moving, he'd figure this out. One foot in front of the other, and before long, he'd be—

Standing a hundred yards outside the hotel.

He had to talk to Alexa.

Too many important decisions, life-altering decisions,

had to be made to let the silence fester and grow to the point where neither would be able to hear the other no matter how much was said.

As his foot hit the first step, a voice called out from one side of the wraparound porch. "Hey, Chance, photo shoot over?"

Chance's hand tightened on the railing as Griffin James stepped out from the shadowy alcove. Despite Alexa's vow that she and the other man were nothing but friends, her words did little to ease the jealousy that had been eating him up inside since Griffin and Alexa had arrived. Not when Griffin was the man she could count on, the man she could trust, the man she'd turned to with the news that she was pregnant with *Chance's* baby.

"Not just the photo shoot," he warned grimly.

"Not just… Ah." The puzzlement cleared from the other man's expression as did his friendly smile. "She told you about the baby, didn't she?"

"My baby," he stated, though just saying the words was enough to make his head spin.

"You might be the baby's father, but there's more to parenthood than biology. Alexa knows that better than anyone."

"What's that supposed to mean?"

"Her own parents barely remembered they had a daughter. They left her behind for one adventure after another until they finally got themselves killed when she was eight."

A child… Her parents had died when she was just a child. She'd spent so much of her childhood without them, growing up alone. And the fear he'd failed to leave behind on the beach clawed at him once more.

I almost died…

Chance clenched his jaw until his back teeth ached. So not funny anymore.

"They cared more about freedom and fun than family," Griffin was saying, accusation slicing through every word. "Sound familiar?"

"I left because of my job." Even to his own ears, the words sounded hollow. "I had an assignment."

"Do you think that mattered to Alexa when she found out she was pregnant and you were gone? Do you think it mattered when she thought you'd been killed?"

The questions were no different from the ones circling through his own mind. He couldn't stop them. Couldn't shut them up. Griffin, though... Chance's hands tightened into fists. He had a pretty good idea how to shut *him* up. "I didn't know she was pregnant. If I had—"

"If you had, then what?" Griffin challenged.

Chance opened his mouth, but when the words wouldn't come, Griffin came to his own conclusion.

"Alexa needs a man who'll be there for her...and for her baby. If that's not going to be you, well, don't be surprised if it ends up being me."

"Like hell!"

"What is wrong with you?" Rory demanded, her eyes narrowed with an anger he hadn't seen since he'd accidently decapitated one of her dolls when they were kids. "What were you thinking?"

Holding an ice bag against his jaw, Chance tried to meet his sister's furious gaze. Not easy to do when his left eye was already swelling shut. Though Griffin James was tougher than he looked, Chance had gotten his blows in. If not for his injured knee, he would have taken the other man down in no time. As it was, Chance didn't know how long they'd grappled together...before they'd both ended up toppling over the railing and falling from the porch.

Bloodied and bruised, the fall knocked the wind out of

them, giving two of the hotel porters the opportunity to break up the fight. Chance didn't know how Rory and Evie heard about it, but as soon as his sister arrived, she had pushed him into Evie's office, out of sight of the guests.

Last he'd seen of Griffin James, Evie had been helping the man to his feet, offering to call a doctor and to comp his stay.

"Griffin James is a guest! What on earth would make you hit him?"

Chance locked his jaw and ducked out of the way as she raised a napkin toward his face. Even when furious, she was still trying to mother him. "We'll be lucky if he doesn't sue! Not to mention the damage this could do the hotel's reputation. Did you even think about that?"

"He deserved it. You have to trust me, Ror." He just wasn't ready to explain all the reasons why.

His sister stared at him. "So in other words, no. You didn't think. You just…acted. To hell with the consequences or with anyone else who might get hurt in the fallout."

Tears glittered in her eyes, and Chance knew this tirade had nothing to do with the fight with Griffin. And the frustration that Chance hadn't come close to burning off rose up.

It's not my fault! he wanted to yell. He hated the hell those reports had put his family through, but he couldn't change what had happened. "Rory—"

"No, don't. Whatever you're going to say, I'm sure I've heard it all before. This is your life, Chance. Go ahead and live like no one else in it matters."

A part of Alexa wanted nothing more than to throw her clothes into her suitcases and book the first flight back to LA. She'd spent far too much of her childhood trying to carve out some tiny piece where she fit in, where she was wanted, where she belonged to force her way into Chance's life.

He wanted her to go back to her world? Fine. Her grandmother had a team of lawyers on retainer. She could hide behind a wall of suits and never have to deal face-to-face with Chance again.

Only she didn't want that. Not for herself or for her child. She didn't want to outsource her emotions or hire other people to fight her battles. She needed to work this out with Chance, to come to some kind of understanding.

She'd dropped a bombshell on him and should have expected to be hit with some of the fallout. Her world wasn't the only one that had been upended since that night in Santa Barbara. At least she'd had some time to come to grips with the news that she was pregnant. She'd given Chance all of five minutes before running off.

Hearing the door to the suite open, Alexa pressed the cool damp washcloth beneath her eyes a final time before hanging it on the towel rack and leaving the bathroom. The last thing she wanted was for Griffin to see that she'd been—

"Griff!" She gasped as she caught sight of him. His dress shirt was untucked, a grass stain marred one shoulder and the front… Bright red blood splattered across the pale blue silk. "My God! What happened? Were you mugged?"

It hardly seemed possible that such a crime would take place in the quaint small town, but she couldn't come up with a better explanation. Rushing to his side, she took his arm. "Did you call the police?"

Griffin waved aside her concern. "No, of course not," he protested, his voice sounding thick and nasally.

Alexa stared down at him as he dropped onto the sofa, his head tilted back against the cushions, a cloth napkin held to his nose as he tried to stop the bleeding. "Why on earth not?"

"Because I didn't think you'd want me to get your boyfriend's ass thrown in jail."

"*Chance* did this? Why?"

Hand still pressed to his nose, he shot her a knowing look. "Why do you think?"

Sinking onto the couch next to him, Alexa could practically hear her grandmother's arch, aristocratic voice echoing in her head.

A Mayhew does not cause a scene.

"I told Chance about the baby, but are you saying he just *jumped* you?"

"Not exactly," Griffin said, only it came out sounding more like *nob exally.*

"Griffin…"

"I might have pushed him into it."

"Why?" Lifting her hands helplessly at her side, she protested, "You were the one who wanted me to tell him about the baby!"

"That doesn't mean I didn't want to punch him in the face for getting you pregnant in the first place."

"Are you okay?"

"I'm fine. Evie McClaren was very solicitous in taking care of me," he said with a rakish wink he couldn't quite pull off thanks to the bright pink bandage across his eyebrow. "I'm pretty sure she's afraid I'm going to sue."

"And…is Chance okay?"

"No worse off than I am. Unfortunately. Although his sister did look like she wanted to kill him, so there's always that."

Alexa dropped her head into her hands with a groan. Great. Now, thanks to her, there was a rift between Chance and his family. "I don't understand why you had to do this."

Sitting up straight, Griffin reached over and pulled her hands down. "Because you deserve a man who's willing to fight for you. And I'm not talking about me."

Alexa's throat tightened with unshed tears, making words impossible…had she even known what to say.

"And now I think it would be best if I head home in the morning."

"You're leaving?" Somehow the squeak of panic escaped the lump in her throat. "But what about the research you were doing for your father?"

"I'm tired of playing by his rules, hoping that what I do will be enough for him to finally hand over my trust fund. Besides, I don't get feeling from either Rory or Evie that they have any interest in selling the hotel. From what I understand, their aunt is the one who makes final decisions, and she's off on some mysterious sabbatical that no one's talking about."

"I don't want you to go," Alexa protested.

"I know. But you need to do this on your own, Allie. I've been holding you back too long."

"Holding me back from what?"

"From taking chances. From spreading your wings."

"I don't know what you're talking about."

"If your grandmother asks you to host an event, who's the first person you call?"

"The caterer."

Griffin's lips twitched. "The second person."

"You," Alexa admitted a little grumpily.

"Right. Because you hate hosting or going to those kinds of events alone."

"And because you're my best friend. You've always been there for me."

"I think I've been there too much. I've become your safety net. You're going through life with me as your plus-one, knowing there's no chance you'll fall in love with me or end up getting hurt."

As much as she wanted to argue, Griffin was right. If he hadn't been overseeing the expansion of one of his family's overseas hotels the weekend of the charity event in Santa Barbara, if he'd instead been at her side as he usually was, she very well might have refused when Chance asked her to dance and certainly wouldn't have taken him back to her room.

"Isn't not getting hurt a good thing?"

"It is, but not if playing it safe keeps you from finding real happiness."

And as much of a mess as her life was currently in, Alexa couldn't bring herself to regret the baby growing inside her... Or the weekend she'd spent in Chance's arms.

"Do you really think I'm going to find that kind of happiness with Chance McClaren?" The words that were supposed to come out in an unbelievable scoff sounded far more wistful.

"I think you found something with him in Santa Barbara."

Alexa shook her head. "I've told you that I wasn't myself that weekend."

"Maybe. Or maybe with Chance, that's exactly who you were always meant to be. He fought for you. Clearly he cares about you. More than he's probably willing to admit. And if you feel the same way, then it's your turn. You need to show you're willing to fight for him."

Alexa had never been one to fight for herself, but to fight for Chance? For their child? That was one battle she had to find the courage to take on.

Chapter Seven

That's exactly who you were always meant to be.

As much as Alexa wanted to pretend she didn't know what Griffin was talking about, she couldn't. For some time she'd wanted to break free of the carefully crafted walls she'd built around her world. She'd lived the past ten years as the face of the Mayhew Foundation, but she wanted to be so much more than that. To be more than a pretty face smiling for the media. To show that she had a mind, a heart, a body. To the public, to her grandmother, to herself…

Somehow Chance had seen that.

Take a chance.

That weekend in Santa Barbara, she'd taken a huge risk. She hadn't wanted to admit it at the time, but she'd opened her heart to Chance only to slam it shut again when he'd left with hardly a moment's notice. And then after the news reports of his death, well, she'd pretty much thrown away the key.

The anniversary party was still going strong—light, laughter and music drifting over to the path that led to the small cottage. She hugged her arms over her chest, wishing she'd thought to wear a sweater. The nighttime temperature would be considered balmy by most people, but Alexa was used to the warmth of Southern California.

The tiny cottage looked even more magical in the faint moonlight, and was the last place she could picture Chance living. But this was only temporary. A place for him to recover before he moved on. She didn't even know if he *had* a permanent residence.

Pushing the troubling thought aside, Alexa hurried up the front steps and knocked on the door. She listened for movement inside but couldn't hear anything over the pounding going on inside her own chest.

Maybe he hadn't come back to the cottage, but if he was in the same shape as Griffin after the fight, she couldn't imagine where else he would want to go.

"Chance?" she called out when he didn't answer after knocking a second time.

Alexa was ready to turn back when she heard a crash from inside. "Chance!"

Heart pounding in her throat, she grabbed the door handle, surprised when the cool metal turned in her hand. She gasped when the door was suddenly pulled open from the inside, jerking her forward and straight into Chance's chest.

His naked, damp chest...

The cottage was dark with only a faint glow coming from the front porch. Swallowing hard, her other senses were overwhelmed by his nearness, the feeling of warm skin over masculine muscles and the scent of soap and shampoo. And despite the desire thrumming through her veins, she couldn't help giving a small laugh.

"What?"

She heard the scowl in his voice as his arms dropped away and he stepped back.

"Lavender."

"What?"

"You smell like lavender."

Chance swore. "I ran out of the soap I brought with me and grabbed whatever my sister had."

The unexpected moment eased some of the tension tightening her chest, and Alexa took her first deep breath since…she found out she was pregnant, it seemed.

"Are you okay? I thought I heard something fall?"

"This place is like a damn china shop. I can't turn around in here without breaking something."

Her heart stuttered as Chance lifted an arm, but instead of reaching for her, he flicked on the wall switch over her shoulder. Griffin's bruises should have prepared her, but she still cringed at the first sight of Chance. The black eye. The swollen jaw.

But try as she might, she couldn't keep her eyes focused on his face. Her gaze lowered to the broad shoulders, muscled arms, the dusting of dark hair over his well-honed chest and abs. The weight Chance had lost since the accident only served to further define every masculine ridge. As if the accident had somehow pared down the man she'd met into this hardened, stark version in front of her.

She took in the drawstring gray cotton shorts, somewhat relieved to realize he hadn't answered the door totally in the buff, and then gasped again when she saw his leg.

"The scars aren't exactly pretty, I know," he said as he turned away from her.

"No, it's not that. It's—" Alexa truthfully was horrified by the violent reminders of what he'd gone through. What he'd *lived* through… But that wasn't what had her grasping his arm. "You need to sit down. Your knee's totally swollen. You should probably see a doctor to make sure—"

"No, no doctors." Despite the implacable tone of his voice, Chance still allowed Alexa to lead him to the feminine floral print couch. "I've seen enough doctors to last me a lifetime."

"Well, maybe you'll think about that before you get in another ill-advised fistfight. For someone so determined to *move on*, you certainly aren't making things easy on yourself."

Chance muttered something that almost sounded like *I'm not the only one*, but Alexa couldn't be sure she'd heard him right.

She reached for a lacy pillow, intending to use it to prop up his leg on the steamer trunk coffee table in front of him, but he caught her wrist. "I was coming to see you." Rolling his eyes, he added, "Both times."

"What?"

"I was coming to see you when Griffin and I got in the fight and just now. I was getting cleaned up so I could come see you without looking like a—"

"A bloody, beat-up mess?"

"Hey, your *good friend* looks as bad as I do."

Alexa shook her head at what was an almost exact repetition of what Griffin had said. "Because that's what's important here."

"You're what's important here," Chance vowed, sending a small thrill through her and his thumb stroked the inside of her wrist. "You and the baby."

Of course. Wasn't that what she had told herself earlier? So she had no reason to feel somehow disappointed that Chance's priorities were exactly where they should be. "Right. The baby." Pulling away from his gentle grasp, she waved her hand toward the doorway leading to the dining room. "I'll go get you an ice pack. The kitchen's…"

Chance nodded. "It's that way."

When he started to push up from the couch, Alexa demanded, "What are you doing?"

"I'm getting dressed. We need to talk."

As if they'd end up doing something else otherwise. Which, considering the difficulty Alexa was having keeping her eyes from straying, might be more of a possibility than she dared to admit… "Good—good idea. I'll, um, be back with the ice pack."

She didn't find an ice pack in the tiny kitchen, but she did spend a good five minutes with her head in the freezer anyway. She pressed a bag of frozen corn to her forehead, foolishly hoping that might cool her heated thoughts as she glanced around.

The kitchen was decorated with the same shabby chic touch as the living room, with white cabinets, an old-fashioned cobalt blue tile countertop and delicate tea saucers decorating the soffit.

Spotting an amber bottle of pills near the sink, Alexa lowered the bag of corn. The prescription was for pain meds as she'd hoped, but judging by the full bottle, Chance hadn't taken any of them. As hard as he was pushing himself with runs on the beach, appointments with physical therapy—oh, and not to mention, ridiculous fights—she couldn't believe he hadn't needed the pills.

Walking back into the tiny living room, Alexa breathed a small sigh of relief to see Chance sprawled against the corner of the couch fully dressed. If only seeing him so relaxed didn't pose a different temptation. His blue-and-gray flannel pajama bottoms and faded T-shirt looked so soft, she wanted nothing more than to cuddle up next to him. To have his arms around her as she rested her head against his chest as they talked about their hopes and dreams for their baby's future.

So simple, and yet so complicated...

She placed the frozen-vegetable bag on his knee before holding out a bottle of water and two of the pills. But Chance was already shaking his head. "I can't take them. They make me...loopy."

"Loopy?"

"Yeah, like a teenager with his first beer buzz. I never know what I'll do or say or... So just forget the pain meds."

"Oh, wow, who would have thought? Chance McClaren, Mr. Live For The Moment, is a control freak."

"That's not true."

"Then take the meds. As long as you take them as prescribed, you'll be okay."

She held his glare for at least a minute, and she could only imagine how much pain he had to be in to grudgingly accept the pills she held out to him. He downed the water, and she tried not to notice how the muscles in his neck worked as he swallowed. Tried not to remember how she'd kissed that very spot as he lowered her to the hotel-room bed for the first time.

"Are you feeling okay?"

Alexa blinked. She was feeling more than a little overheated, but could Chance actually see those thoughts written on her face?

"You know, morning sickness or whatever?"

"Oh, that. No, not anymore." Perching on the edge of the sofa cushions, she added, "I get tired easily, and I'm starving half the time, but I feel fine."

"And the baby's healthy?"

A hint of vulnerability in his blue eyes had Alexa's heart softening. "The baby's fine."

"I wish you would have told me sooner."

"Chance…"

"I—I'm trying to understand why you didn't, but seeing you here with Griffin… I've acted like a total ass."

"I told you Griffin's just a friend."

"A friend you were thinking of marrying."

"Yes."

"Are you still?" The plastic bottle crackled as Chance's fingers flexed.

"Still what?"

"Still thinking?"

"No, Griffin's leaving in the morning."

"Can't say I'll be sorry to see the guy go."

Alexa opened her mouth to argue only to stop. How would she have felt if she'd arrived in Clearville to find Chance almost engaged? Even to a woman he considered just a friend? Simply imagining a beautiful woman on Chance's arm had jealousy digging deep.

"I am sorry. I should have been up-front about Griffin and the baby from the start. It's just that seeing you here was such a shock especially after—"

"Those damn news reports." Chance sighed as he dropped his head back against the cushion. Leading Alexa to stare at that spot on his throat once more…

Jerking her gaze away, she clasped her hands between her knees. "I honestly did try to get ahold of you once I found out I was pregnant."

"Before the bombing."

"Yes."

"But not after."

"No," she admitted. "After that first report, I didn't know what to think, how to feel. I was just starting to get used to the idea of being pregnant, and then I had to face the thought of raising a child on my own."

"And after?" he pressed.

"And after…after I'd read that you were alive, that your condition was improving, I didn't know what to believe. What if those reports were wrong, too?"

Pushing back against the couch cushions, he sat forward as he met her gaze. "I'm not going to lie. My job comes with risks, but *life* comes with risks. It's not as dangerous as you might think."

"The scars on your knee tell a different story." She spoke again when he would have protested. "And it's more than a job. You're willing to go where not every journalist will go and tell the stories that not every journalist will tell."

Truthfully, Alexa had been drawn to his work before she'd been drawn to the man himself. The night of the charity event, she'd been so impressed that she'd spoken to an acquaintance of her grandmother's, Roslynn St. Clare, about a possible showing for the talented Chance McClaren.

Knowing Chance as she did now, Alexa realized that a gallery showing filled with wealthy patrons and patronizing critics was hardly his style. He preferred to stay on the front line and let his work speak for itself.

"You have a true calling, and I admire that."

"You admire me, and yet you think I'm the type of man who wouldn't want to know he had a child, who wouldn't take responsibility."

Alexa squeezed her hands tighter together. Maybe that was what she was afraid of. Not that Chance would walk away from their child, but that he would stay. Grimly determined and duty bound to do the right thing. She didn't know which was worse—a father who was never around or one who was there but wanted to be somewhere else.

"A child should be more than a responsibility. A child needs to know he or she is wanted, loved… What?" she demanded when she noticed him studying her with a sympathetic expression on his face.

"Just thinking of something Griffin said," he murmured.

Alexa raised an eyebrow. "You mean the two of you actually talked and didn't just start pummeling each other?"

"We did a little of both."

And he clearly wasn't going to tell her what Griffin had said. Which, knowing her friend, could have been just about anything.

Chance leaned his head back again, and Alexa could see some of the tension draining from his body as exhaustion and the pain pills started to take over. "I should go. You need to rest."

She settled her hands against the cushions, ready to push to her feet, but without opening his eyes, Chance reached out and caught her wrist. "Stay," he encouraged.

Her heart suddenly pounding in her throat, Alexa swallowed. Heat radiated from the simple touch of his skin against hers, tiny flames of memory licking to life in its wake.

"I don't think that's a good idea. You should rest."

Chance's eyes opened as he leaned toward her, his movements languid and purposeful at the same time. "I haven't had a good night's sleep since the last time you were in my bed. I can't close my eyes without imagining you there."

Alexa stared at him, dumbfounded. He'd thought about her while he was away? Imagined her by his side, even while they were apart? Those same thoughts, memories, *desires* haunted her dreams, but to think Chance had felt the same way, felt that same longing…

"Chance." His name was a breathless gasp of air as he rose above her and pulled her to her feet. Her legs trembled, and Alexa knew she should leave before it was too late.

But it had been too late from the first time she'd spotted him from across the ballroom. When he'd caught her very much in the act of doing something a Mayhew did not do—interfering with one of her grandmother's biggest donors by diverting the inebriated man's unwanted attention from a young female server.

And Chance McClaren had been watching her all along. But instead of seeing disappointment or disapproval in his gaze, his blue eyes had glowed with amusement and admiration.

But that was then. This was now. So much had changed and yet one thing hadn't changed at all. She wanted him to kiss her now as desperately as she had then.

"Alexa. *Lexi.*" The nickname sent shivers down her spine. To the rest of the world, she was Alexa Mayhew. Only Chance called her Lexi. Only Chance…

Her name was still on his lips when he claimed hers in a kiss, and she buried her fingers in his hair as he pulled her body tight to his.

They were a perfect fit, the muscled strength of one of his thighs between the softness of hers, the curves of her breasts against the wide plane of his chest, the subtle roundness of her belly cradled by his concave stomach.

Their *baby* cradled between them.

Startled by the thought, Alexa jerked back. Her chest heaving as she gasped for much-needed breath, she stuttered, "That's not— We can't—" Swallowing against the arousal she saw reflected in Chance's taut expression, she said, "This is a bad idea."

He stared at her for a long moment before shocking her with a laugh. His white teeth flashed in the first genuine smile she'd seen since she arrived. "That's what you said in Santa Barbara, too."

"Yes, well, this time I mean it."

Her pulse quickened as he stepped forward and erased the hard-fought distance she'd placed between them. "Bad ideas. Ask anyone, I'm full of 'em."

For a brief moment a shadow crossed his features before his expression cleared. Reaching up, he touched the butterfly hairpin in her hair. "My good-luck charm," he murmured.

Alexa swallowed. Though a still-smoldering desire lingered in his eyes, his gaze was slightly unfocused, as well. "You really weren't kidding about the effect pain meds have on you, were you?"

His half smile was teasing, sexy and, yes, the slightest bit loopy. "Told ya."

Ignoring the disappointment coursing through her, she said, "Which is why you need to go to bed. Alone," she stressed, reminding herself as much as Chance. The chemistry, the attraction, the desire to feel his body pressed against hers once more had her resolve trembling right along with her suddenly rubbery legs.

"Not like I can get you more pregnant."

No, no danger there. But the risk that she'd fall even further for him? That was a very real—and very frightening—possibility. "Yes, well, as romantic a proposition as that is, I'm still not sleeping with you."

He gave a sigh heavy enough to stir the hair at her temple, but allowed her to guide him down the hall. With an arm draped over her shoulders, he leaned on her enough for Alexa to wonder if he really had done further damage to his leg. But when he pulled her tighter to his side and pressed a kiss against the top of her head, she wasn't sure if she was holding him up or if he was simply holding her.

With the faint glow from the living room, Alexa had the impression of a very girlie bedroom, complete with

canopied lace-trimmed bed. Chance was so not the typical Sleeping Beauty and yet…"Get some sleep."

But before Alexa realized what he planned, he fell back
on the mattress…taking her right with him.

"Chance!" Her protest was cut short as she landed on
top of him with an inelegant grunt. "What are you doing?"

Rolling with her on the bed, he pinned her to the mattress with a firm arm wrapped around her waist and
warm, heavy thigh between her legs. Alexa sank into soft,
wildflower-scented sheets, a feminine contrast to Chance's
hard, masculine body above hers.

"I told you. I can't sleep without you."

"And I think I told you, I'm not sleeping with you.
Chance?" Alexa pushed at his shoulders, her hands sliding uselessly against soft material of his T-shirt and the
smooth muscles beneath. "Chance!"

She may well have questioned the truth of his words,
especially given what he'd told her about his aversion to
pain pills, but actions spoke louder as he settled deeper
into the pillows with a contented sigh and promptly fell
asleep…with her.

Chance knew he was dreaming again.

The dream was so realistic—like the ones in the hospital during the first days after his surgery. He could feel
the silken brush of Alexa's hair across his arm, the teasing warmth of her breath against his neck. He pulled her
closer, but instead of bare skin against his, he encountered
the softness of some fuzzy material.

Why was she wearing clothes? His dreams always
started with her naked in his arms and ended with her
slipping away…

"Chance! Chance, wake up!"

He ignored the voice, the one that sounded like Alexa's

but was only a trick. He tightened his grip, determined not to let her get away and equally determined not to wake up. When he opened his eyes, she would be gone.

"Seriously, Chance. I can't breathe here."

"Dreams don't need to breathe," he protested, rolling until he half pinned Alexa's dream self beneath his body.

She laughed at that—maybe a little breathlessly—before saying his name.

With his eyes still closed, his lips found the sensitive spot where her shoulder met her neck. She smelled just like he remembered—something sweetly floral but with that hidden hint of spice. She whispered his name again, even more breathlessly this time, and heat flooded through his veins.

In the real world, too much stood between them for Chance to give into desire. The secret she had kept, the uncertainty of the future, the responsibility of their child. But this was a dream where nothing could come between them.

Nothing but that stupid fuzzy sweater.

"Why are you wearing clothes in my dream?" he complained.

Alexa groaned, sounding as frustrated by the unnecessary clothing as he was. But when she spoke this time, a note of panic entered her voice. "Chance, you need to wake up now." She pushed at his shoulders, but he wouldn't budge. "No, really, you need to wake up. I think someone's here!"

He faintly heard a car door slam, something else completely out of place in his dream and enough to make him wonder... The sound, combined with a sharp pain in his leg as Alexa scrambled out from beneath him, jerked him from the remnants of slumber.

Blinking, he stared at Alexa as she scurried off the side of the bed. With a wide-eyed glance at the window, she straightened the cashmere sweater from his dream and smoothed her hair. Not that it helped. Her clothes were wrinkled, her normally perfect hair tousled, her face free of makeup and still softened from sleep.

His heart did some kind of a slow roll inside his chest. He'd never seen her look more beautiful, and he asked himself again how the hell he'd managed to walk out of that hotel room four months ago.

Was it any wonder he'd pictured her there a hundred times since, and yet for the life of him, he couldn't figure out...

"What were you doing in my bed?"

"What was I— You—" Color bloomed in her cheeks and she shook her head in exasperation. "Do not start with me this morning. And get up! Someone is here!"

What the hell happened last night? He remembered the fight, Alexa showing up at the cottage, taking those damn pain pills... After that, things got a little blurry, but considering she was fully dressed and he—Chance tossed back the covers to confirm—yep, he was wearing a T-shirt and a pair of flannel pajama bottoms, he was pretty sure nothing had happened while she was there.

His reflexes slowed by his still groggy state of mind, he barely blinked as a pair of jeans hit him in the chest and then fell to the floor in a heap. "What—"

"Get dressed," Alexa hissed as she turned toward the open closet door.

He swallowed a groan as he awkwardly bent to snatch the jeans from the floor. "Who's here?"

"I have no idea, but someone—" The knock on the front door interrupted the flurry of activity as she clutched one of his shirts to her chest, her eyes wide with panic.

After a split second of silence, the knock sounded again. "Chance, sweetie!"

Alexa still didn't move, but Chance saw her eyes narrow at the sound of the feminine voice. "Sweetie?"

This time he didn't even try to swallow his groan. He almost wished he had some past girlfriend standing on his front porch as Alexa clearly suspected. "That's my mom," he sighed. Limping over, he grabbed the shirt from her frozen hands. "Prepare to meet the parents."

Chapter Eight

"Your parents?" Alexa's voice rose an octave as the knocking on the front door suddenly seemed to reverberate inside her chest. "I can't meet your parents now!"

She had no experience with anything like this. Not even as a teenager had she been caught in a compromising situation.

A Mayhew does not sneak boys into her bedroom or make out in the back seat of a car.

His gaze washed over her from head to toe. "You could meet the queen of England like this. You look as beautiful as ever."

Heat rose in her cheeks at the compliment as well as at the intimacy of the moment. Even though they'd spent a weekend together, even though they'd made love, an even more powerful connection stretched between them. An unspoken acknowledgment that said they were in this together.

The truth was, she could have left his bed at any time last night. Though he had initially held her tight, the pain pills weren't enough to keep him from a restless sleep. Before long, he'd rolled to his side and then tossed onto his back. She'd even pushed back the covers, ready to slip away, when he called out her name.

At first she thought he was awake, only to quickly realize he was still asleep and reaching out for her in his dreams. "Don't go. Don't leave…again."

And in that moment, she'd known she wasn't going anywhere.

He'd needed her last night, and as impossible as the idea sounded in her own mind, Alexa couldn't shake the thought that Chance needed her now.

His dark hair was mussed, and a pillow crease lined one lean cheek. His morning beard combined with the black-and-blue bruises on his jaw and eye gave him a dangerous air. But there was something almost defensive in his posture even as he joked, "There's always the window if we want to try to make a break for it."

"We? They're your parents," she reminded him.

Chance sighed. "Exactly."

After tossing the clothes onto the bed, he reached for the hem of his T-shirt. Alexa's jaw dropped as he stripped off the shirt and tossed it aside. "What—what are you doing?"

"Hey, you wanted me to get dressed. And it's not like it's anything you haven't seen before."

Seen, felt, tasted… Her face heated even as she protested, "Not with your parents right outside the door!"

His deep chuckle sent another round of nerves dancing in her stomach. "Better than right inside the door… which is where my mother will be in about two seconds if I don't get out there."

"They're going to think we're sleeping together."

"They're gonna *know* once they find out about the baby."

He laughed again when Alexa spun around the second his hands dropped to the drawstring waistband of his flannel pajamas. But memory supplied such mouthwatering detail she almost wondered why she'd denied herself.

The rustle of denim was loud in the otherwise silent room, the rasp of the zipper seeming to run straight down her spine. The hair on her neck stood on end as Chance stepped close enough to murmur in her ear, "I'll try to buy you a few minutes."

"To duck out the window?"

"Or join us in the living room. Up to you."

Alexa used the extra few minutes in the bathroom to wash her face and brush her hair before stepping into the living room, where Chance made the briefest of introductions.

Dozens of unspoken questions were written in his parents' eyes, and it would have been impossible to miss the look the older McClarens exchanged in the split second before Alexa held out her hand.

Chance's mother, Mary, ignored it, enveloping Alexa in a quick hug. Familiar brilliant blue eyes beamed as she said, "It's so good to meet you. I'd like to say Chance has told us so much about you, but he's always been notoriously silent when it comes to his love life."

"Mom…"

Mary met her son's pained protest with an exasperated look. "Well, it's true. We haven't met one of your girlfriends since—"

"So what are you two doing here?" Chance interrupted, silencing his mother but certainly not Alexa's curiosity about the last woman he'd brought home.

"We're heading down to Santa Rosa for a retirement

party for an old friend of your father's," Mary explained as she started tidying the small room, straightening a ruffled pillow, picking up the empty water bottle, pausing only slightly at the now-defrosted bag of corn. "We thought we'd stop by since it's on the way."

"Not exactly on the way," her husband muttered, jingling a set of keys in the pocket of his khakis.

Matthew McClaren had salt-and-pepper hair and the same wide forehead and strong jaw as his son, but classic bone structure wasn't the only similarity between the two men. Alexa hadn't missed the stubborn set to those matching jaws.

Mary, however, smoothed over the moment with a laugh. "It is if you take the scenic route."

"Still," Chance pointed out, "you have a long drive ahead of you—"

"Which is why we left before the crack of dawn. We certainly have time for a late breakfast with the two of you while we're here."

"There was an anniversary party at the hotel last night. The restaurant's bound to be packed right now."

His mother waved aside the warning. "No offense to Hillcrest's restaurant, but you know we've never been big on eating out. Rory told me she made sure to stock the kitchen before you came?"

"Packed to the rafters," Chance answered wryly.

"Perfect! Alexa, you'll lend me a hand, won't you? We'll let the men talk," Mary said with a pointed look at the two males in question.

"I, um, sure," Alexa said weakly with a final glance at Chance before following Mary into the kitchen. She knew perfectly well why she was nervous about a one-on-one chat with Chance's mother. What she couldn't figure out was why Chance seemed just as uncomfortable talking man-to-man with his own father.

Despite her initial concerns, Alexa felt instantly at ease with Mary McClaren. Partly, she imagined, because the older woman kept a constant stream of conversation flowing. Her mouth moved almost as fast as her hands as she bustled around the tiny kitchen, slowing only when she had to search another cupboard or two for an ingredient.

"I am sorry we just showed up out of the blue like this. If Chance had told us— But, well, Chance doesn't say much of anything when it comes to his personal life."

Alexa paused, the plate in her hand hovering an inch above the pale oak table as she waited for Mary to say something more about the woman in Chance's past. But when nothing more was forthcoming, she admitted, "My own arrival was somewhat of a surprise, as well. I've only been in town for a few days."

"But you and Chance..."

"Met a few months ago in Santa Barbara. We, um, planned to keep in touch after he left for another assignment but then—"

Alexa cut herself off as Mary's movements slowed to a stop. She bowed her head for a moment as they both silently acknowledged what happened—what almost happened— *then*...

"You do like pancakes, don't you?" Mary asked Alexa over her shoulder, her smile forcefully bright. "So many people nowadays have food allergies."

"No, no allergies." She couldn't recall the last time she had pancakes, though, more likely to have something as simple as tea and toast in the morning. And during her bout with morning sickness, even that had often been too much. But now... Finished setting the table, Alexa walked over to the counter. Her stomach let out a very unladylike growl as Mary dropped a handful of blueberries into the batter and gave a quick stir with a wooden spoon.

"I don't think I've ever seen someone make pancakes without a recipe before. Other than a professional chef."

"Professional?" Mary gave a laugh. "You mean like those cooks on television? Oh, trust me. I'm not in their league. I guess I've just been doing it for so many years I can make them automatically."

Alexa hadn't been talking about television. She'd been referring to the full-time chef on her grandmother's staff. Her face heated slightly at her near faux pas. If Mary didn't think of herself in league with a TV personality who could smile for the camera and beat an egg at the same time, she certainly would have felt outclassed compared to the cordon bleu–trained chef her grandmother employed.

"So if you don't consider yourself a professional, how did you learn all this?"

"I guess I consider myself a professional mom. Not always the most glamorous of jobs and not one that will win you an award, but rewarding enough for me." With her reddish-brown hair streaked with gray and faint lines fanning out from her hazel eyes, Mary McClaren exuded a warmth and comfort that drew Alexa in.

A professional mom. She liked the sound of that. For the past few months, she'd been so caught up in the idea of being pregnant, of having a baby, somehow the thought of being a mother had gotten lost. "So you learned all this after Chance and Rory were born?"

"Oh, no! My own mother taught me to cook when I was still a little girl. It was always such a treat to be with her in the kitchen."

"Oh. Right." Of course. These were skills Alexa was

already supposed to have. All things her mother was supposed to have taught her.

"By the time I had two kids, I barely had time to breathe. Thank goodness this was all second nature by then. Although with a newborn, then the trick came in learning how to do it all one-handed."

"One-handed?"

"It's amazing how quickly you figure out how to hold an infant in one arm and still crack eggs with your free hand."

Alexa swallowed a disbelieving laugh. Holding a baby while cracking eggs. Sure, she'd give that a try. Right after—oh, who knows? Sword swallowing? Fire juggling?

"But then once the kids were older, I was able to pass down all I'd learned. Rory was such a good little student, standing on a stool by my side, so eager to help. I think for Chance, it was more about the bonus of licking batter from the beaters and having first dibs on dessert." Mary's eyes sparkled at the memory. "So what kind of things did your mother teach you?"

Her mother taught her how to smile even when she was crying inside.

You be a good girl for nanny and Mommy will be back soon!

Bree didn't like when Alexa cried when she left or begged her not to go. So Alexa learned to be a good girl, always waiting hopefully for her mother to return.

That hiding behind a smile came in handy as she said, "Oh, my mother taught me so much, it's hard to know where to begin."

But as she watched Mary in the kitchen, Alexa couldn't help thinking that the most important lesson Bree had taught her was how *not* to be a mother.

A lesson Alexa had just over five months to totally unlearn.

* * *

"So how did the two of you meet?"

Chance didn't even try to hold back his groan. "Five seconds, Mom. That must be some kind of record."

His mother had whipped up a feast of blueberry pancakes, maple syrup, scrambled eggs and bacon. The tiny table could barely hold all the serving dishes and plates, and despite the sweet smells filling the kitchen, he didn't have much of an appetite.

Not when he was going to end up getting grilled as the main course.

She gave him a reproachful look as she passed the butter to his father. "It's just a question."

And hardly one that was out of line. Especially not when coming from parents who had just walked in on their son scrambling out of bed with a young woman.

Even if nothing had happened the night before. Which was both a relief and an embarrassment. He'd learned way back as a kid that he and pain pills didn't mix. He'd had plenty of cause to take them during the daring exploits of his youth, and the side effects were never pretty. Walking in his sleep. Talking in his sleep.

Hell, he could only imagine what Alexa had to put up with. Snippets of memory floated through his mind, but it was too similar to what had occurred after the accident, when most of what he recalled had been nothing but imagination.

Alexa's warm, feminine curves beneath his body... Her golden hair spread out across the pillow... Her slender arms around his neck...

I'm here, Chance. I'm right here. I won't leave you.

One thing he knew wasn't imagination or some kind of delusion.

Alexa was pregnant. With his baby. He was still coming to grips with the sudden turn his life had taken.

"We met at a charity event," Alexa was saying to his all-ears mother, her movements graceful and precise as she used a knife and fork to cut her single pancake into tiny bite-size pieces. "Chance was there to sign some of his photographs as part of a silent auction."

Chance's grip tightened on his fork. Alexa couldn't possibly know the minefield she'd just walked into. His job was a decade-old point of contention between him and his parents. His father, especially, and Chance didn't miss the scowl on the elder McClaren's face.

Let the McClaren men talk.

As if his mother didn't know perfectly well that he and his father got along so much better when they weren't talking.

Chance shoved another big forkful of fluffy, melt-on-your-tongue, buttery pancake into his mouth. If he could keep his mouth shut—or full—for a few minutes more, they might all get through this visit unscathed.

He'd done his best to hide his sigh of relief when his mother offered the destination for their trip. His father would be eager to get back on the road, every turn and stop carefully plotted along the way, despite what Mary had said about taking the scenic route.

He swallowed a snort of laughter at that. His dad never took the scenic route. Matthew McClaren was direct to a fault, always on the straight and narrow, never one for taking the road less traveled.

Chance had known from the time he was a kid that getting lost was the best way to find himself. To find out what he was capable of, to find out what he truly needed and wanted out of life.

Discovering that what he wanted was the exact opposite of what his parents wanted for him? Well, that was a hurdle the three of them had yet to successfully cross.

"Chance's work drew some of the highest bids that evening. I can't tell you how many people would pay a small fortune for a McClaren original."

Matthew gave a grunt, the dismissive sound that much more abrasive compared to the pride in Alexa's voice.

Pride? She'd made it clear how she felt about his job and its dangers, and yet...

Sitting by his side at the tiny table, Alexa offered him a small smile. "I would have bid on one of them myself if winning wouldn't have seemed unfair."

"Unfair? Why would it?" Mary asked.

"I had organized the event, so it was best that I not win any of the items. You know, for appearance's sake."

For appearance's sake... She'd told him that night how much she hated living her life with that kind of scrutiny. How she longed to be free. She hadn't told him she'd thought about bidding on his photographs.

He wondered what she and his mother had talked about in the kitchen. His mother wanted nothing more than to see him settled down and married. Hell, she'd been the only one in the family to approve of Lisette. Even Rory, who almost always looked for the best in people, called her his crazy ex-girlfriend.

But for Mary, all she cared about was that while he and Lisette had been together, he'd spent more of his time focusing on *his girlfriend's* career rather than on his own dangerous one.

"Well, I hope you were able to take some kind of memento home from the event."

His gaze met Alexa's, this time her smile more than a little wry. "Oh, yes, I definitely brought something home with me."

A baby. *His* baby.

And while a part of him still wanted to reject a reality he wasn't ready to face, another, bigger part of him wanted to reach over and pull Alexa into his arms. It was the same feeling he'd had that morning while she was throwing clothes at him in the bedroom.

A feeling of connection…

For a man who'd lived his adult life without ties to hold him down, the emotion should have scared the crap out of him. And yet he wasn't willing to break the fragile contact, letting the moment lengthen and strengthen between them.

Until his father interrupted when he demanded, "So what's with the black eye?"

"You know me, Dad, always the one picking a fight."

His father didn't miss the subtle dig judging by the way his grip tightened on his fork.

"Chance, you—"

"It was my fault," Alexa jumped in suddenly. "The fight—everything—was my fault."

His father raised an eyebrow as he glanced over in surprise, almost as if noticing Alexa for the first time. Not that Chance bought into that for a second. Even wearing yesterday's clothes and without a speck of makeup, she looked stunning. With her head held high as she took on his father, defending Chance, she was even more beautiful than the first time he saw her.

Too beautiful for words, and certainly too beautiful to be so easily dismissed as his father waved off her claim. "Unless you're a lot stronger than you look, something tells me there's more to the story."

Before Chance could shove back from the table, Alexa placed a hand on his flexed arm and gave a reassuring squeeze. "There is," she agreed as she glanced from his father to his mother and back again. "It was mostly just

a big misunderstanding, but when it comes down to it…
Chance was looking out for me."

Jealousy still carved a hole in his gut when he thought
of Alexa and Griffin together. Friends, just friends, she
had said, but it was still a blow knowing Griffin was the
man she had turned to. The man she could trust, the man
she could count on. Griffin. And not Chance.

Griffin had been willing to marry her, to prove he was
responsible—when Chance was responsible. For Alexa.
For the baby they had created together.

"So, does this mean the two of you are…serious?" His
father speared him with a knowing look, expecting the
typical answer.

*I'm not ready to settle down. My career comes first. A
family isn't part of my future.*

Alexa had held her own with his father, but now her
hand slid away from his arm and her attention fell to her
mostly empty plate. Immediately missing the contact,
Chance reached over and laced her slender fingers through
his own. As he met her startled gaze, he couldn't help but
think, *Ready or not.*

"I wouldn't call it a 'thing' between us. More like a
baby. And if you'll excuse us, I have a wedding…to photograph."

Chapter Nine

"I now pronounce you husband and wife. You may kiss your bride."

Chance took a deep breath, leaned forward…and lifted his camera for the perfect shot.

The guests gathered in front of the gazebo burst into applause as the newly married couple exchanged their first kiss, and he gave a silent exclamation of his own as he captured the moment with a click of a button.

He'd done it. His first wedding. He hadn't expected it to be so nerve-racking. He didn't know how his sister put up with this week after week.

From his own admittedly ignorant and totally biased view from behind the camera, Chance thought Rory had done an amazing job on the simple afternoon wedding. Red-and-white-flowered garland draped the gazebo's pillars and railing. Matching velvet bows decorated the tie-backs of the chairs on either side of the white lace runner that led to the platform steps.

Even the weather—frequently rainy and overcast in November—had cooperated. The sun had peeked out from behind the clouds during the ceremony, shining down on the tuxedoed groom and his vision-in-white bride. The party would move into Hillcrest's ballroom for the reception, but for now...

He focused on the couple as they made their way down the aisle amid a shower of red rose petals. He didn't doubt the pictures would be perfect, but he still couldn't shake the dizzying feeling of vertigo every time he looked through the lens.

He was totally out of his element, and he knew it. But it was more than that. It was looking through the lens and trying his damnedest not to imagine Alexa in a white gown and flowing veil. Alexa walking down the aisle, bouquet in hand. Alexa repeating the vows, tears filling her beautiful eyes as she promised to love, honor and cherish.

Only just yesterday, she'd been thinking about saying those very words to her good friend Griffin. And even though she'd reassured him she was not accepting the other man's proposal, Chance still couldn't make the leap of seeing himself as the groom. What did he know about being a husband?

What did he know about being a father?

That was the question his father had demanded after Chance dropped his bombshell about the baby. His mother had been over the moon, instantly ready to share what sounded to him like horror stories about pregnancy woes and labor pains and sleepless nights filled with round-the-clock feedings.

But it was his father's words that stuck with Chance.

How do you plan to parent a child from half a world away? Fatherhood isn't something you can phone in like your latest story.

Chance didn't have any answers. He wasn't ready to walk away from his career, but after having Alexa back in his life for only the past few days, he damn sure wasn't ready to walk away from her or their baby.

They had time to work out the details. It was what he'd told his parents before ushering them out of the cottage even as his mother instructed him to keep them up to date on things like the baby shower, the baby's due date, and oh, yeah, by the way, the date of their *wedding*.

Judging by the way Alexa's eyes had widened at his mother's words, Chance figured she was looking for the nearest window to jump out of.

Sucking in a deep breath, he lifted the camera, taking comfort in the familiar weight in his hands. Wondering as he often did how the most important thing he and his father had in common, the one thing they both loved, was also the one thing that had driven such a wedge between them.

He worked for another half hour, taking shots of the bridal party posed on the gazebo platform and lining the steps. But every damn time he had to blink away the image of Alexa standing there— Good God, was that really just the day before? How was it that his life had completely changed in a mere twenty-four hours?

The muscles in his leg burned in protest as he bent to a knee for an angled shot of the bride and groom, reminding him that life didn't need hours. It could change in a split second. Still, it was a relief when the bride announced they were ready to join the guests for the reception.

"Did you get the shot?"

"Did I get the shot?" Forcing a confident smile he was far from feeling, Chance turned and snapped a quick photo of his sister, who glared in return. "Don't you know who you're talking to?"

"Yeah, my obnoxious older brother."

"Hey, I'm here, aren't I? I even got that haircut you wanted."

"Right, and the black eye's a wonderful addition."

Despite the words, Rory's tone was more exasperated than angry. They hadn't had much time to talk since he'd arrived. Rory, busy with the finishing touches before the ceremony started, and Chance with photographing the bride in the moments leading up to the wedding.

"I take it you talked to Mom and Dad."

"Are you kidding? I was *grilled* by Mom and Dad, who seem to think I should have known everything that was going on when clearly I didn't have a clue!" Taking him by the arm, she led him away from the gazebo and toward a curve in the tree-lined path leading back to the hotel, she asked, "Alexa's pregnant?" At his nod, she added, "And the baby's yours?"

"Was that a question?"

"I think it's a somewhat legitimate one." She shook her head at his scowl. "No pun intended. But, Chance, she was engaged to another man."

"He's just a friend."

"And you believe that?"

Chance's shoulders tightened though he couldn't blame Rory for her doubts. His track record with women was far from stellar. Lisette had manipulated him more thoroughly and professionally than the physical therapist who worked on his leg. He supposed he should be grateful she'd been so determined to claw her way to the top of the fashion world. No way would she have risked her figure or her future by getting pregnant—not even as a way to keep a hold on her favorite photographer.

"Why would Alexa lie, Rory?" He pulled up short as he confronted her suspicions. "If she was going to trick someone, Alexa would be better off fooling Griffin James into believing he's the father. The guy's family has almost as much money as Alexa's does."

Chance made a decent living. He'd invested well, and his nomadic lifestyle limited his spending when it came to worldly possessions. But his bank account was pocket change compared to the Mayhew and James fortunes.

"Look, I did some research online about Alexa."

"Oh, good, because you know you can always believe anything you read on the internet."

Ignoring him, Rory said, "She lives with her grandmother who's something of a recluse. I saw pictures of their home. It's this walled fortress of a place, Chance. It wouldn't surprise me if they have armed guards at the gate."

"What's your point, Rory?"

"I'm just saying, it will be a lot easier for you two to work things out here than back home on her turf."

"Her turf? You make it sound like some kind of battle." He thought of Alexa's wealth, of the dozens of lawyers she could easily employ, the miles of red tape she could use to keep him away from their child. Away from her... It was a battle he couldn't afford to win.

Chance swallowed. It was a battle he couldn't afford to lose.

A high-pitched whistle sounded, and Rory pulled her phone from a pocket in the pale yellow skirt she wore. Her dark brows pulled tight as she read the message on the screen.

"What is it?" Chance asked. "Some kind of wedding crisis?"

His sister shook her head. "I guess that would depend on you."

"What are you talking about?"

"Evie just sent a text." Rory held up her cell. "Alexa's checked out of the hotel."

* * *

Alexa had spent her entire adult life trying to live up to her grandmother's standards, but she was seconds away from throwing a tantrum that would make any reality-star diva proud.

"Griffin James checked out earlier today," she stressed to the wide-eyed maid who stood in the middle of the hotel suite, cleaning cart at hand. "I am still here."

Though why she was still there was rather fuzzy at the moment. Or maybe that was just due to the tears she refused to let fall.

If she had any question about how Chance felt about their baby, he'd made his answer loud and clear.

Alexa would be better off fooling Griffin James into believing he's the father.

Her head had been spinning since meeting Chance's parents that morning, and with Chance busy with the wedding, Alexa had gone back to the suite to say goodbye to Griffin. She'd given him a brief recap of all that had happened, tempted to smack him when he wouldn't stop laughing during her explanation of how the McClarens had all but walked in on her and Chance.

"We still have a lot to discuss—including the fact that his parents are clearly expecting us to get married—but I'm glad I told him about the baby," she'd told Griffin, believing in her heart that things were going to work out somehow.

Now she didn't know what to believe.

"I'm sorry, ma'am," the maid was saying, "but I was told to ready this room for a new guest who will be checking in this evening. Maybe the front desk can help?"

Alexa didn't want to go back down to the lobby. She wanted nothing more than to bury her head in a pillow and cry. But the recently fluffed and perfectly arranged pillows were no longer for her use. She was no longer a guest and had no reason to stay in Clearville. No reason not to return home.

"My luggage... My clothes... Where?"

"I'm sure the front desk..."

"Right." Swallowing her tears, Alexa straightened her shoulders and left the suite only to bump into a solid masculine form in the hallway. "Oh, I'm sorry. I'm—"

"Crying." Chance caught her by the shoulders and ducked his head to get a good look at her face. "Why are you crying?"

Concern furrowed his forehead, the expression on his face sending her already confused emotions into another tailspin. "I'm not— I don't—"

"Come on, let's go back to the room."

"It's not my room. You have a new guest arriving tonight."

The arm he'd wrapped around her waist tensed. "You've checked out?"

"Evidently."

Guiding her back into the suite, he made eye contact with the startled maid. "Out." The one word had the poor girl dropping her dust rag and scurrying out of the suite with her cart in tow.

Dropping onto the blue-and-white-patterned love seat, Alexa stared at the empty doorway. "Do you know what people would say about me if I treated the staff like that?"

"I don't care what people say."

"No, of course not." Alexa cared. Maybe that was part of the problem. Maybe she cared too much. About things people said. About things she overheard...

"Look, Alexa." Chance ran a hand through his dark hair to grip the back of his neck. "Don't go, okay?"

She blinked up at him, the words not the ones she expected to hear. "You want me to stay?"

Dropping onto the cushion beside her, he reached for her hand. "Of course I want you to stay. When I heard you were checking out…"

She shook her head. "I'm not. There was a mix-up with the room."

"We'll figure it out. We'll figure all of this out."

The words were so similar to the ones she'd used earlier, and she wanted to cling to that promise and yet… "Do you really wish I'd tried to fool Griffin into thinking this baby was his?"

"What? No, Alexa!" His hands tightened around hers. "You were there? You heard…that?"

"I went to find you." Remembering why she'd gone to look for Chance, Alexa slipped her hands from his to wrap her arms around her waist. The wild swing of emotions rushed back—from exhilarated to devastated—in the blink of an eye. "I thought I felt the baby move. It's still so early, I can't even be sure, and it's not like you could feel it anyway—"

Her words cut off with a gasp as he reached over, his large palm laying claim to the slight swell of her belly. And Alexa suddenly hoped he *couldn't* feel what was going on inside her body as yearning grew from everywhere his hand touched to everywhere it *didn't*.

"I'm glad this baby is mine, Alexa." Possessiveness and a familiar heat burned in his blue eyes. "What you heard me say to Rory… I guess I'm worried you might still think Griffin would be a better bet as a father."

"As soon as I felt—or at least thought I felt—the baby move, I wanted to share that with you, Chance." Covering his hand with her own, she pressed his palm tighter against her belly, strengthening the already miraculous bond between them. "With *you*, not with Griffin."

"So you'll stay?"

"The room—"

"We'll talk to Evie and figure something out." After reaching into his pocket, he held out his closed fist. "Besides, Cinderella, you don't want to leave this behind, do you?"

She gave a small laugh when she saw the butterfly pin resting in his palm. "Again?"

"You seem to be making a habit of leaving this in my bed."

Feeling the heat rising to her cheeks, she reached out, but Chance's hand closed around hers. "And you seem to be making a habit of finding me and giving it back."

"Lucky thing."

"Last night at the cottage, you said the pin was your good-luck charm."

Chance groaned and immediately let her go. "I told you I'm an idiot on pain meds. Who knows what I was talking about?"

Alexa had the feeling he knew exactly but that he didn't want to explain. As she fingered the fragile butterfly, she tried not to think about a time when Chance's luck might run out.

"When my brother invited you to come down to the reception, I don't think cleanup duty was what he had in mind."

Alexa paused, drink tray in hand, to glance over her shoulder. Rory McClaren held two dessert plates loaded down with wedges of chocolate and raspberry cream cake. "I don't mind lending a hand."

Her plan to simply watch the festivities from the sidelines hadn't lasted long. Sitting toward the back of the ballroom, she'd admired the rose and gerbera daisy centerpieces on each white-clothed table. Matching red velvet bows decorated the back of every chair, the bright color a complement to the ballroom's dark walnut wainscot. She'd been content to watch and laugh at the sight of couples young and old strutting their stuff to the "Chicken Dance" on the parquet inlaid dance floor.

But when the music changed to a romantic ballad and the bride's seventysomething grandfather asked her to dance, Alexa hadn't had the heart to refuse the sweet man. That dance was followed by one with the groom's preteen and adorably serious nephew. No one minded that she wasn't an invited guest, and each time she looked Chance's way, he met her glance with a quick wink of his camera flash.

She couldn't help but watch him throughout the reception as he smiled and laughed with the guests and bridal party, helping even the most reluctant subject relax in front of his lens.

That was the Chance Alexa remembered from Santa Barbara. Charming, funny, with a confidence she found undeniably sexy.

But she'd seen another side of him, too, during the unrehearsed shots when the bride and groom or wedding guests didn't realize he had them in his sights. A serious, determined side. The camera seemed like a part of him in those moments as his focus narrowed and the world around him disappeared.

That must be what he was like in the field. When he would shut off his emotions with the single-minded purpose of getting his shot. When bombs could go off around him and he wouldn't even notice.

"I've never coordinated a wedding, but I know what it's like to plan for large events. There's always something that needs to be done."

Now the reception was starting to wind down. The band

still played to a handful of couples on the dance floor, but most of the guests had left. The Hillcrest House staff had started to discreetly move around the ballroom, sweeping away empty plates and glasses from the white-clothed tables. Not one to sit around when there was work to be done, Alexa had grabbed a tray to help out.

"When it comes to weddings, there's always too much work, but if you're lucky, sometimes there's too much cake. Like a piece?"

At Alexa's nod, Rory set the plates on a nearby table before sinking into a chair with a groan. "My feet are killing me. One of these days, I'm going to start wearing tennis shoes to these things."

Chance's sister looked professional yet eminently approachable in a yellow shirtwaist dress with cap sleeves. Her kitten-heeled slingbacks matched perfectly, and Alexa couldn't imagine her sacrificing style for comfort, no matter how much her feet hurt.

Alexa took a small bite of cake, and rolled her eyes as the rich chocolate and tart fruit flavor melted in her mouth. "This is to die for."

"All our cakes are made by a local baker who owns a café on Main Street called Sugar & Spice. You should check it out while you're in town. I mean, if you're staying?"

Rory's prying was somewhat more subtle than Mary's, but Alexa could certainly see a mother-daughter resemblance. "I'm staying for now, but I have a fund-raising benefit at the end of the month. I'll need to be back in LA by then."

"Chance mentioned the work you do. I can't imagine all the preparation that must go into coordinating those star-studded events." She waved her fork at the ballroom. "I'm somewhat new at all of this. A part of me is still surprised when everything goes off without a hitch."

"I've organized more benefit dinners and charity events than I can count. The only way those events succeed is to rely heavily on volunteers, which means being shorthanded more often than not. I've set tables, arranged flowers, help prep in the kitchen. I've even—"

She laughed at a long-ago memory, the sound drawing a curious look from Rory. "Even what?"

"Back when I was still a teenager, my grandmother hosted a party at the house. The singer she'd hired canceled at the last minute." Alexa shook her head. "And my grandmother, in her infinite wisdom, decided I should fill in as the night's entertainment."

Rory's dark eyebrows rose. "You can sing?"

"After all the countless hours with a private music instructor, you—like my grandmother—would think so," she said wryly. "One good thing to come out of that disaster was that it did put an end to those lessons."

The brunette fought a smile as she dug in for another forkful of the moist, decadent cake, and Alexa strangely felt like she'd passed some kind of test.

"You know, it's been years since I've met one of Chance's girlfriends."

Bonding over bridezillas and celebrity nightmares wasn't enough for Alexa to feel comfortable confessing she wasn't Chance's girlfriend. More like a weekend stand—if such a thing existed.

So instead, she murmured, "Your mother might have mentioned something along those lines this morning."

Rory grinned. "That must have been fun."

"I'd likely use another word for it."

"His last girlfriend did a real number on him. Jerked him around enough in their six months together to give him a permanent case of relationship whiplash." Her tone was easy, but Alexa didn't miss the weight behind it.

"I'm not here to jerk Chance around." Remembering what the wedding coordinator said during their first meeting—about magic and romance—Alexa said, "I'm sorry for not being more up-front about my…history with Chance. I'm sure the next couple who comes through will find their Hillcrest House happily-ever-after."

"Final dance, folks!" the lead singer called out from the small stage in the corner of the room. "Make it last."

An older couple joined the younger kids on the dance floor, including the groom's nephew who had found a dance partner closer to his own age.

"Don't give up on your own happily-ever-after so soon, Alexa," Rory advised with a speculative smile. "Something tells me your story isn't over yet."

Alexa turned in the chair, following the other woman's gaze, and felt her heart skip a beat. Walking up behind her, Chance held out his hand. "Can I have this dance?"

Chapter Ten

Chance's pulse pounded in his veins as Alexa placed her slender hand in his. He'd been dying to hold her in his arms again since… Since she'd joined him at the reception? Since she'd arrived in Clearville? Since he'd left her hotel room four months ago?

He knew the answer was all of the above. And after watching her tonight, he wanted her even more.

She'd been as charming and gracious at this small-town wedding for a couple she didn't even know as she'd been at the celebrity gala in Santa Barbara. He'd watched her make an old man feel young again and make a young boy feel like a man as she'd moved so gracefully in their arms.

Both of her partners had beamed with pleasure and pride as she'd easily smoothed over any of their missteps. Though Chance had every confidence in his own abilities, he didn't doubt the same smile was tugging at his lips.

She was amazing, and the most incredible part was that she didn't even seem to know it.

"You're staring," she accused as she ducked her head slightly and kept her gaze focused on the top button of his shirt.

"I know. It's hard not to when you're the most beautiful woman here."

Anyone could see that, but Chance suddenly realized how often that was all anyone saw. *The face of the foundation...* That was how Alexa had referred to herself, as if beauty was all she had to offer.

"Do you know the first thing that attracted me to you that night in Santa Barbara?"

Alexa blinked up at him, and Chance could tell she didn't know how to answer the question. She had beauty, wealth, sophistication, but so too had many of the women there that night.

As the hostess for the charity event, she'd greeted every wealthy donor by name, welcoming them with a flawless grace. But as he'd watched, he quickly recognized the strength behind the beauty.

"It was seeing how you handled that drunk jerk."

A small smile tugged her lips. "That drunk jerk is one of my grandmother's biggest donors, and a high-tech billionaire."

"Doesn't change the fact that he was drunk jerk. I saw him proposition that server, and I was ready to toss him out on his fat wallet."

"That would have been something to see."

"Yeah, but it might have gotten me thrown out of the event and taken the focus away from all the hard work you'd done for the charity. But you—you were a pro. You handled him so perfectly that the guy didn't even know he was being handled. He handed over a donation and was back in his limo before he knew what hit him."

"It's all part of the job."

"You know it was more than that. You could have notified security, but that might have caused a scene and even more embarrassment for the poor girl." He brushed a strand of hair back from her cheek, mesmerized by the softness of her skin, by the silkiness of her hair. By her...

"That night, I thought you looked like an angel, but the truth is you're human, just like the rest of us, but with a heart of gold. You care about people. And that's—that's what I saw that night. That's what you've shown me again here today."

She shook her head, and that same wayward strand of hair fell forward to tempt him again. "I haven't done anything special today."

"You made your dance partners' days just by saying yes. You've made my day—" his week, his month, his year "—just by saying yes to this dance."

"Thank you, but still... As a wedding photographer, you should know that no one is more beautiful than the bride on her wedding day," she chided gently, and just like when he'd lifted his camera earlier, the images in his brain jumbled together.

Alexa... The bride... Alexa, the most beautiful bride...

"Oh, Chance." Seated with him at a table in the now empty ballroom, Alexa looked up from the wedding pictures he'd uploaded to his tablet. She stopped at an image of the bride adjusting her veil in front of a full-length mirror. Sunlight shone through a side window, casting an aura around the blond-haired woman. "She looks like an angel. This picture is perfect."

"I still need to do some editing," he said, deflecting her praise, but she wouldn't hear of it.

"It's perfect," she repeated.

She'd seen some of his award-winning photos, including the ones he'd donated the night of the charity auction. Those images were raw, stark, brutally honest. So she could understand his concerns that his professional eye might not translate to capturing the hope and romance of a young couple's wedding day.

He needn't have worried.

He shifted at her side, uncomfortable with her praise as she swiped through the next photos. Her breath caught at a picture of a toddler flower girl in a ruffled red dress, her white wicker basket held upside down over her head. Flipping through the pictures quickly, Alexa could view a near live-action video of the little girl's adorably unsteady march down the aisle—her blond corkscrew curls bouncing, her blue eyes bright with laughter, her chubby cheeks almost matching the color of her dress.

In the last photo, the little girl was grinning straight at the camera. Seeing that little girl through Chance's camera lens, through *his* eyes, had her own blurring with tears.

"Weddings are supposed to make you cry. Not looking at wedding pictures. Especially not pictures of people you don't even know." His voice was as gruff as if he, too, was fighting some overwhelming emotion.

"I don't know these people, but— These pictures, seeing them, makes me feel like I'm seeing the real you."

"Funny." Chance gave a soft laugh. "Every time I lifted my camera, I felt like I was seeing you."

"Seeing me?" Puzzled, Alexa set the tablet aside. A different kind of longing gripped her as she met his gaze. She felt like they were back on the dance floor. Despite the slow song, her head had spun dizzily, a feeling that stayed with her even after the music stopped. He overwhelmed her every sense—from the low rumble of his voice, to the scent of his woodsy aftershave, to the brush of his muscular thighs against hers… With his lips mere inches above hers, she'd wanted nothing more than to kiss him again.

She hadn't abandoned the list of "a Mayhew does nots" to the point where she'd be comfortable making out on a dance floor—even an almost empty dance floor.

But the longing and the head-spinning, pulse-pounding desire was still there, reflected back in Chance's handsome face as he brushed a lock of hair back behind her ear. A shiver ran down her spine as he said, "I kept seeing you dressed in white, walking down that aisle, wearing a veil."

Her breath seized in her chest. Her heart beat so loudly against her breastbone she wondered that he couldn't hear it. Surely he couldn't be saying what she thought he was saying? "Chance…"

His smile was wry as he reached up to touch her hairpin. "It wasn't just this butterfly I carried with me all those months. It was you…Lexi."

"We barely know each other!"

"The baby you're carrying goes to show we know each other pretty well."

"Not well enough to—" Alexa couldn't bring herself to say the words.

"Get married?"

Oh, good Lord, he was saying what she thought he was saying!

"Look, I know your parents clearly expect us to get married but—"

"This isn't about what my parents want. It's about me wanting our child to have two parents. For the three of us to be a family."

"Our child does have two parents. Getting married doesn't make you a father."

A muscle in his jaw thrummed. "Getting you pregnant doesn't make me a father either. It takes more than that."

"You're right. It takes caring and commitment—"

"Which is why I want to marry you. To prove to you that I am committed—to you and to our baby. We have a responsibility to do what's best for our child."

Alexa couldn't deny the sincerity or seriousness of his vow. If only he didn't sound like he was trying to convince himself as much as he was trying to convince her.

And it had to be some kind of record, right? To be proposed to by two different men within a two-month period with neither one of them mentioning the *L* word.

She hadn't expected it from Griffin, and it was foolish to think she'd hear it from Chance, and yet somehow she still had...

"So we get married and then what? Do you realize I don't even know where you live?"

"I have an apartment in LA, but we can live wherever you want. That doesn't matter."

"Doesn't matter?" she echoed faintly. She supposed it didn't, not when so much of his life was on the road and everything he owned fit in a beat-up backpack. Something that clearly wouldn't change even if it meant leaving a child—or wife—behind.

"What matters most is that I want to be part of our child's life."

"And how would that work when you're halfway around the world?" Putting himself in God knew how much danger...

"That's not fair, Alexa. That's my job. A job I love."

Ah, and there was the *L* word missing from his proposal, given instead as a reason why he would always be walking away.

"You're an amazing photographer, but the assignments you take—the risks. I was serious about the money people would be willing to pay for your photographs, Chance. I spoke with Roslynn St. Clare. She's a friend of my grand-mother's, and she owns one of the most prestigious art galleries in Beverly Hills. And she was *interested* in your work."

But he was already shaking his head. "That's not me, Alexa. That's not who I am, and even if I wanted to do a show with Roslynn St. Clare, I couldn't."

Even though she hadn't expected him to agree, the sting of disappointment burned the back of her eyes. "Why not?"

"Because I would never know if she was asking for me or if she was asking for you…" At her confused frown, he added, "A friend of your grandmother's, remember? I imagine that friendship pulls a lot of weight."

"If you think I used my family's influence to persuade Roslynn, I swear to you, Chance, I didn't!"

He sighed. "You may not have intended to, but I'd never know for sure, would I?" He shook his head. "I don't know how we went from talking about getting married to talking about my job, but we need to focus on the future. Our future."

And Alexa didn't know how he could talk about *his* career and *their* future as if they were two completely separate things. "I made a mistake in not telling you I was pregnant right away, but I'm not going to keep you from our child. You can be in his or her life as much—" or she feared as little "—as you want. We don't need to get married for that to happen."

"When Griffin asked you to marry him, you said you'd think about it." He cut her protest off with a pointed look. "At least do me the same favor."

"All right," she said finally, not that her agreement was much of a concession. As lacking as his proposal was, she doubted she'd be able to push it from her mind. "I'll think about it."

"And you'll stay in Clearville until the end of the month?" he pressed.

Alexa nodded. "I'll stay."

"She can't stay." Evie stared at him from across the marble reception desk. "When the room opened up, we offered it to another guest. And with the anniversary party last night and the wedding today..." She shrugged a shoulder. "We're booked."

Chance narrowed his gaze as he took in his cousin's enigmatic expression. His short time in Clearville had either already dulled his edge or she was one hell of a poker player. He prided himself on his ability to correctly read a source, knowing at times his life depended on it. And yet he had no idea if Evie was telling the truth.

He didn't even know if she was trying to get rid of Alexa or hoping to push her into his arms.

If the latter was part of Evie's plan, she—hell, *they*—had their work cut out for them.

Chance had never imagined proposing to a woman, which might have something to do with why he'd screwed it up so royally. All that talk about responsibility and commitment... He probably couldn't blame Alexa for refusing to marry him. Not when even to his own ears, it sounded like his *dad* was the one proposing.

He was still sticking with his plan to marry Alexa, to give their child two parents. He just needed her to get on board, and to do that he needed to keep her in town for the next three weeks like she'd promised.

Rubbing his aching forehead, he tried to hold on to his temper. "Evie, I swear if this is some kind of a con—"

"The rooms are full. If you want to go around banging on every door in the place, you can, but I wouldn't recommend it." Tucking a strand of her blunt-cut dark hair behind an ear, she added, "Besides, I don't know what you're all bent out of shape about. She can always stay at the cottage. From what Rory tells me, that's where Alexa spent *last* night."

Family... Sometimes he didn't know if he wanted to throttle them or... Oh, yeah, throttle them.

"I really don't think this is a good idea," Alexa protested, and not for the first time as Chance maneuvered up the steps to the cottage, her designer luggage in each hand and under both of his arms. He'd insisted on carrying her bags, and she felt ridiculously embarrassed for having overpacked.

Honestly, why had she thought she needed to bring so much with her?

So, in spite of his protest, she hurried across the porch to open the front door before Chance tried to somehow do that himself, too.

"You shared a suite with your good friend Griffin," he pointed out as he dumped her bags in the middle of the living room and turned on one of the Tiffany lamps.

"That's different."

"Not sure I see how."

"Probably because Griffin's never seen me naked!" As soon as the words burst from her lips, a flush rose in her cheeks. "I cannot believe I just said that."

Amused, Chance said, "Well, I'm glad to hear it. And it's not like we aren't even. You've already seen me naked, too. Plus, you're the one who said we barely know each other. I can't think of a better way to become more intimately acquainted than to live together."

Alexa didn't think she'd imagined the way he stressed *intimately*, and the spike in her heart rate was exactly why staying with Chance was entirely different from rooming with Griffin.

"Besides, it's late. Do you really want to start calling hotels to see if they have a room available?"

"If you had told me earlier, I would have had more time."

But after Chance came back from talking to Evie, he hadn't said anything about the hotel being full. Just like he hadn't said anything more about getting married, confirming Alexa's belief that he regretted his impulsive proposal.

Instead, he'd taken her to dinner at Hillcrest's elegant dining room, where he'd asked about the kind of food her obstetrician recommended and if she'd had any cravings. She told him about her sudden hunger for big, juicy hamburgers and her love of mint chip ice cream, and he laughed when she confessed that particular craving might have predated her pregnancy.

And it hit her in that moment that by keeping the pregnancy a secret, Chance wasn't the only one who had missed out. She'd also robbed herself of someone with whom to share all the tiny details.

So when he carefully repeated, "If I had told you earlier…" Alexa immediately felt the heavy weight of guilt press on her shoulders.

Catching sight of her stricken expression, Chance swore beneath his breath. "I shouldn't have said that. What's done is done, and what we need to do now is to focus on the baby and how to move on from here. Look, it's been a long day. Let's get some sleep, and if you want to find someplace else to stay, we can talk about it in the morning."

Alexa had to admit she was exhausted. She was also very much aware that the tiny cottage had only one bedroom… and one bed. "I'll, um, sleep on the sofa. You'll be more comfortable in the bed."

Chance shook his head. "Forget it. I rarely sleep through the night anyway."

"You did last night," she reminded him.

His eyes glowed at the memory. "That's because you were there with me."

Chapter Eleven

Chance didn't argue with Alexa's insistence on sleeping on the sofa. Instead, he simply waited. After the long and emotional day, she fell asleep with her head on his shoulder as they watched television. He made the most of the opportunity, lifting her into his arms and carrying her to his bedroom.

He fully expected her to wake up, but the pregnancy must have taken more out of her than she wanted to admit. Other than a soft sigh that had goose bumps rising over every inch of his body, she didn't stir. She snuggled deep into the covers when he placed her in the center of the mattress, and Chance gritted his teeth as he resisted the urge to join her there.

Next time they ended up in bed, he wanted them both awake and aware of the undeniable desire drawing them together.

She'd still been sleeping when he'd left for a physical therapy appointment that morning. His therapist had shaken his head at the sight of his bruises but reassured Chance that his rehab was progressing. He'd been on his way back when he received a text from Rory, asking him to stop by the hotel.

But when he showed up, Rory was busy with the arrival of her fiancé, Jamison Porter, and his daughter, Hannah. Settling into one of the overstuffed lobby chairs to wait, Chance froze when the little girl climbed right into his lap despite the multiple empty seats around him.

"Um, hey, Hannah."

The blond-haired girl giggled. "Hay is for horses, Uncle Chance. I don't have a horse. I have a dolly. See?"

Her body a warm, bubblegum-scented weight, she settled against his chest and right into his heart. "Um, that's nice?"

"Miss Rory gots her for me after I was a flower girl in Miss Lindsay's wedding. I had a basket and I threw flowers and I wore a crown in my hair. Now I get to be a flower girl for my daddy's wedding to Miss Rory! An' after the wedding, Miss Rory will be my next mom!"

His head spinning from the rapid-fire conversation, Chance glanced up as Rory walked over. "Next mom?"

His sister smiled indulgently at her soon-to-be step-daughter. "Four-year-old logic for what it means to get a stepmother," she explained. "Which if you think about it, actually makes more sense as a description."

As far as Chance was concerned, none of the babbled conversation made sense. He fought back a groan as Hannah handed him the doll to play with.

"You should be thanking me," Rory told him. "This will be good practice for you."

The longer Hannah babbled on, the less he understood. Something about dolls or maybe dogs or— He didn't know what. By the time she scrambled off his lap, narrowly missing the family jewels with a deadly knee, he was exhausted.

Something that evidently showed, based on Rory's gleeful laughter. "Oh, my gosh! The look on your face. I don't think I've ever seen my big brother so scared! And of a little girl and her doll, of all things!"

"I have no idea what she was talking about," he admitted.

"She's four, Chance. It's not rocket science," Rory said as she sat beside him. "She was telling you about her dolls and how Jamison built her a miniature gazebo like the one here on the grounds where her dolls can play."

"And she thought I'd want to know about that…why?"

"Because she's *four*," Rory repeated. "Her dolls are important to her, and she wants them to be important to you because you are also important to her."

"She doesn't even know me."

"You're her Uncle Chance. She adores you. Evie, too, although I'm not always sure why since Evie's never been kid friendly."

"And I am?"

"In your own way, yeah. You love adventure, excitement, exploration, and that's what being a kid is all about."

Chance smiled. Rory was right. He'd loved being a kid. There were some parts he'd never outgrown.

"And besides, you're having a baby. By the time your child is Hannah's age, you'll have tons of experience at being a dad." After a slight hesitation, she added, "I talked to Alexa a little at the reception last night. She says she's only staying through the end of the month."

"That's right."

Pointing out what he already knew, she said, "That's

not much time. So what are you going to do? You can't just let her leave."

"I can't exactly force her to stay."

"I'm not talking about forcing. I'm talking about *persuading*."

"That didn't exactly work either," he muttered.

"You asked her to stay?"

"I asked her to marry me."

Rory's jaw dropped in utter shock. "Seriously? You proposed? When? How?"

"Last night, and what do you mean how?" Chance shifted uncomfortably, rubbing at the back of his neck where his collar—hell, his own damn skin—felt too tight.

"Were there flowers? Music? A ring?"

Only if he counted the ones for another couple's wedding.

Throwing her hands up in exasperation, Rory said, "Honestly, Chance, you can't ask a woman to marry you in some kind of knee-jerk reaction and expect her to say yes. Didn't you see Alexa at the reception, willing to dance with perfect strangers just to make them smile? This is a woman who's looking for romance and longing for a man to sweep her off her feet."

The last time Chance opened his heart to romance, Lisette had stomped all over it. What kind of fool would he be if he left himself open for that kind of heartbreak again?

"Morning."

A shiver ran down Alexa's spine at the sound of Chance's voice. She glanced over her shoulder to find him lounging in the kitchen doorway. How was it he could look so good after rolling out of bed to go straight to a physical therapy appointment? Dressed in a faded T-shirt and navy sweatpants, his dark hair mussed from the workout session, stubble shadowing his jaw along with a rainbow of bruises, and her mouth still went dry at the sight of him.

She wrapped her hands around a fragrant mug of peppermint tea, holding on to the warm ceramic to keep from reaching out as he stepped into her personal space and made it his own. "How was your appointment?"

"Good. My therapist says I'm ahead of schedule." He frowned, and she could only imagine his frustration that even ahead of schedule wasn't healing fast enough. "How'd you sleep last night?"

"Better than expected, considering I went to sleep on the couch and somehow woke up in your bed." A hint of annoyance filled her voice, left over from the frustration of his scent, his warmth, his presence invading her subconscious with dreams that left her restless, achy and, as it turned out, alone.

But instead of owning up to what he'd done, Chance had the nerve to grin. "Do you have a habit of sleepwalking?"

"Hardly. I told you, you should take the bed."

"And I told you…I'm not sleeping there without you."

Heat flooded her cheeks, and Alexa only wished she could blame it on the steam rising from her mug. Even though she told herself that giving in to sexual chemistry wasn't a solution, she wasn't sure how much longer it would be before she would be asking him to join her there.

Breaking the sensual spell, Chance glanced over her shoulder at the kitchen counter. "What's all this?" he asked, gesturing to her tablet propped up against the toaster.

The video tutorial she'd been watching while brewing her tea had run its course, the television chef now paused and waiting to be played back. Alexa had hoped to have breakfast made by the time he returned from his therapy appointment. But unlike his mother, she needed a recipe.

She'd been astounded by the overwhelming number of results for something as simple as blueberry pancakes.

Which, as it turned out, might not be so simple after all...

"Do you realize if you type 'blueberry pancake recipes' into a search engine, you get more than two and half million hits?" Two and a half *million*, and she'd never made a single one.

Not seeming nearly as amazed by this revelation, Chance chuckled. "Blueberry pancakes again? Is this some kind of pregnancy craving?"

"I thought you liked pancakes."

"I do, although maybe not for breakfast every day."

"When your mother was here, she talked about cooking for you and Rory when you were kids. About how the two of you would stand on step stools on either side of her and argue over who got to lick the batter from the spatula."

"Yeah, my mom loves to cook, and she always wanted to share that love with us. I hadn't thought about that in a long time." His voice faded off into forgotten memories as he murmured, "Too long..."

Alexa didn't have those kinds of memories of her mother, had precious few memories of her parents at all. "This is the part where I should probably tell you I don't actually know how to make pancakes." Embarrassed by that admission, she added, "We always had a chef on staff," which only made it sound that much worse.

Because her family hadn't stopped at hiring chefs, and it wasn't only her lack of skill as a cook that had Alexa doubting her ability to be the kind of mother their child deserved...

"Hey." Reaching out, Chance took the tea mug from her hands and set it aside to pull her into his arms. With his forehead against hers, he said, "As an annoying and occasionally wise woman reminded me just this morning, we're not having a full-grown kid. We're having a baby. It will be months before that baby is old enough to be eating pancakes, and years before the baby'll be old enough to stand on a step stool by your side to lick the batter from a spatula. We have time to figure this out, to figure *all* of this out."

With her hands fisted in the soft cotton of Chance's T-shirt, Alexa couldn't decide if it was wonderful or scary how easily he read her thoughts. Settling on *wonderfully scary*, she asked, "So what do we do now?"

"Now, we make pancakes. The old-fashioned way." After powering down her tablet, he reached into a cupboard over the stove and pulled out a small blue-and-white-striped tin box.

"What is that?"

"Copies of my mother's recipes." His smile was more than a little wry as he said, "If we're going to learn how to do this, we might as well learn from one of the best."

"Alexa, you're right on time!"

Rory greeted her with a smile as she crossed the lobby. The pretty brunette was dressed for the season in a brown V-neck sweater and plaid burnt-orange skirt. But the warm colors, like the fall decorations, only served as a reminder that Thanksgiving and the end of the month were drawing near.

We have time to figure this out.

Alexa couldn't help the small smile that came to her lips. After some trial and error, and quite a bit of laughter, they had figured out pancakes. She'd waited breathlessly as he took the first taste before proclaiming, "Best pancakes ever."

And when he held out his fork for her to try the buttery, maple-soaked goodness, a different kind of anticipation caught inside her chest as a different kind of hunger sharpened his expression. Alexa wasn't sure how she managed to swallow a single bite, let alone to finish an entire pancake. Recalling the expression about not being able to take the heat, she had quickly gotten out of the kitchen.

She'd spent the morning on the phone with Raquel after informing Virginia that she was extending her stay until the end of the month.

"A Mayhew does not abandon her duties, Alexa."

"I know, and I'm not. I'll check in every day, and I'll be back before the benefit," she'd promised.

Her grandmother had been far from pleased, and Alexa feared she would be even less so once she told her about her pregnancy.

But Alexa wasn't ready for that conversation, and she'd been surprised and relieved when Rory had called her later in the day to invite her to lunch with some friends. Alexa didn't think she could start another cooking lesson with Chance in the kitchen that didn't end in the bedroom.

Wanting to make a good impression, Alexa had debated over what to wear, trying to find a balance between too dressy and, well, way too dressy. Despite the ridiculous amount of luggage she'd brought with her, her expanding waistline was starting to limit her options.

Finally, after the third outfit change, Chance had caught her by the shoulders on the way back to the bedroom.

"What are you doing?" he'd asked.

She waved a hand at the wide-legged burgundy slacks she wore with an ivory scoop-necked sweater and multicolor, knitted scarf. "I need to change."

"Why? You're perfect just the way you are. Relax, Lexi. You don't have to be the face of the foundation. Just be *you*," he had encouraged her.

Keeping that in mind, Alexa took a deep breath and smiled at his sister. "Thank you for inviting me."

"We're heading into town for lunch at Sugar & Spice," Rory told her.

Recalling that the café was owned by the baker who supplied Hillcrest House's wedding cakes, Alexa said, "I'll be sure to save room for dessert."

"It's better to play things safe," a slender honey-blond woman said as she joined them. "I've been known to order dessert first."

"Alexa, this is Lindsay Kincaid, and Sophia Cameron will be here as soon as she's done chasing down Kyle."

"Chasing—" Alexa started at the unexpected feel of something tugging at her burgundy slacks. No, not something. Someone, she realized as she glanced down into a chubby-cheeked face and big dark eyes.

"Looks like you found Kyle." Rory bent at the waist to offer a four-fingered wave at the baby. "Or he found you."

"This is Kyle?" The little boy who'd pulled himself unsteadily to his feet wore a long-sleeved red T-shirt beneath the most adorable pair of denim overalls. A bit of demand entered his babbling as he slapped a dimpled hand against her leg.

"He's not walking on his own yet, but he's the fastest thing on all fours," Lindsay laughed.

A particularly exuberant pat had the boy losing his grip. He teetered for a moment before toppling over and landing on the patterned carpet. Looking a bit stunned, the baby stared up at Alexa for a moment before those big eyes stared to fill.

"Oh, sweetie. It's okay. Don't cry!" Without stopping to think, Alexa bent and scooped up the little boy. He was heavier and studier than she expected as he settled into her arms.

Despite the tears dampening his long lashes, the little boy rewarded her with a drooly smile, showing off two shiny white bottom teeth. The baby patted her shoulder this time, and as ridiculous as it was, Alexa couldn't help but feel like she'd received a stamp of approval.

Five months. In five months, I'll be holding my baby. Our baby.

"Honestly, I don't know how I am going to keep up with him once he starts walking!" A petite dark-haired woman with a huge diaper bag strapped to one shoulder crossed the lobby to join them. Her dark eyes and pixie haircut immediately identified her as the boy's mother. "He only recently learned to crawl, and now every time I turn around, he's broken some speed record in getting away from me."

Handing the little boy to his mother, Alexa said, "He is so cute."

"Thank you. I'm Sophia Cameron, and you've already met Kyle." She bounced the baby in her arms, eliciting a gurgling laugh that had them all smiling.

"I've asked Alexa to join us for lunch."

"The more the merrier," Sophia said, smiling her welcome. "So long as you don't mind this guy coming along. My babysitter canceled at the last minute."

"Of course not. He is so cute..." Noticing the other women exchanging smiles, Alexa felt her face heat. "I already said that, didn't I?"

"You did. Do you have children?" Sophia asked innocently.

Alexa froze, aware of Rory's gaze on her. She wasn't sure how much Chance had told his sister but figured she wasn't revealing any secrets when she said, "Actually, I'm pregnant."

"Oh, how exciting!" Sophia exclaimed.

"Congratulations, Alexa," Lindsay offered.

"It gets even better," Rory added with a grin. "Not only is Alexa going to be a mother, but I'm going to be her baby's aunt."

The two women squealed again, hugging not just Rory but also Alexa. Their exuberance caught her off guard as did the sudden rush of emotion. Sophia was the first to notice. "Oh, my goodness. Are you okay?"

"I'm fine." Alexa wiped at the tears on her cheeks, feeling extremely foolish for breaking down. "It's just—"

The first time anyone had been truly happy to hear about the baby.

Her shock at discovering she was pregnant had barely worn off when the news reports had announced Chance's "death." And then she'd made such a mess of telling him he was going to be a father. She couldn't go back and do things differently, but going forward...

"I'm happy," she told the other women. "I'm crying because I'm happy if that makes any sense at all."

"Are you kidding?" Sophia asked with an understanding smile. "Welcome to my world. When Kyle got his first tooth, I went from overjoyed at how big he's getting to devastated that he's growing up too fast in an instant."

"Alexa."

The deep voice rang out across the lobby, and she glanced up to see Chance striding toward them, an intense look on his handsome face. Reaching her side, he all but glared at the three women around her. "What's wrong?"

She blinked at him, dislodging a lingering tear, and said, "I was about to ask you the same thing."

"Me?" His brows pulled together over the brilliant blue of his eyes. "I'm not the one who's crying."

Butterflies fluttered in Alexa's stomach as he reached out to brush a thumb beneath her eye. Catching his hand in hers, she promised, "I'm fine, Chance. It was just, well, hormones."

His gaze searched hers as if searching for the truth to her words. Seeming satisfied with what he saw there, he stunned her a little by pressing a kiss to her forehead. "If you're sure you're okay."

"She's coming with us to lunch, big brother, where we promise the only tears will be ones of ecstasy over to-die-for desserts. That's assuming you'll let her come out and play."

He didn't appear the least bit embarrassed by his sister's teasing, and as he feathered his fingers through Alexa's hair, the sights and sounds of the elegant lobby faded away until only the two of them existed...

When Chance had entered the walnut-paneled lobby and saw that Alexa had been crying, his overriding instinct had been to rush to her side. Only once he realized she was fine did his focus expand, taking in the smug smile on Rory's face, the two wide-eyed women beside her and the grinning, dark-haired baby one of them held.

"Da-da!" the little boy shouted, his chubby arms reaching out toward Chance.

"Whoa! Hang on there, kid." Catching the boy as he practically dive-bombed from his mother's arms, he murmured, "I'm not a daddy yet."

Although that wasn't entirely true. He was already a father to the unborn child Alexa carried, but it still didn't feel entirely real. The baby was just an idea, a concept he had yet to wrap his mind around. Nothing as substantial as this little guy currently wrapped around his neck.

But when he saw the watery, tender smile on Alexa's face as she reached out to touch the baby's soft cheek before brushing her fingers across his own bristled jaw, the emotional blow was real enough to leave him weak at the knees.

His sister's laughter broke the moment, and she said, "Sophia, Lindsay, this is my brother, Chance. The baby magnet."

Not too long ago, Chance would likely have been annoyed at his sister's teasing. But now… The wonder of it all had him smiling even as the little boy's responding grin had drool running from his dimpled chin and soaking into Chance's T-shirt.

A bit of baby slobber couldn't hurt, and the kid really was cute…

"Da-da!"

"Looks like little Kyle here knows how to spot 'em," Rory said as she patted Chance's soggy shoulder.

"From the moment he was born, Kyle's been a daddy's boy. But Jake's been traveling a lot lately. You miss your daddy, don't you?"

"Da-da!"

His mother laughed at what sounded like a firm agreement. "It is his favorite word, and one that can pretty much mean anything, including a name for big, masculine men."

"No need to apologize. Really," he said, handing the boy back with a surprising amount of reluctance.

As Alexa asked Sophia a question about Kyle, Chance could already see how Rory's friends had accepted her. She smiled and laughed with the other women, and seemed as fascinated by little Kyle as he was, reaching over more than once to grasp the baby's hand or to adjust the strap of his tiny overalls.

"Thanks for inviting Alexa," he told his sister quietly. "I appreciate you making the effort."

"I like her. And I have to admit, I wasn't sure I would, considering your past taste in women."

"Alexa is nothing like Lisette," he argued. And yet hadn't he had doubts of his own, questioning if she'd used her wealth and status to try to get him that gallery showing for his work?

Lisette had been a master at manipulation, going behind his back and working behind the scenes to make sure he was offered jobs at star-studded events and along red-carpet runways, but always for her own benefit.

He couldn't deny that Alexa's motives were pure and unselfish, but her efforts still made him wonder if she could ever accept him for the man he was.

His editor had called again to let Chance know he'd been given the green light on a follow-up to an article he'd written on a refugee camp in Serbia—if he was ready to get back to the job.

"Three weeks," he'd heard himself say to the other man.

Alexa had given him three weeks before she planned to go back to LA, the same amount of time he had to convince her that he could be a husband, a father and a photojournalist.

He watched as Sophia pulled a toy from the large diaper bag hooked to her shoulder. With the boy focused on the stuffed dinosaur, she swooped in to wipe his glistening chin with a small cloth, her movements easy and efficient.

When Kyle reached out again, this time to Alexa, a beatific smile curved her lips as she caught his pudgy hand and pressed a kiss to his palm. He babbled happily as she entertained him with a game of peekaboo using her scarf. Making the little boy belly laugh and making Chance... He didn't know how to describe the sucker-punch feeling inside.

"She's so good with him," he murmured. "She's going to be an amazing mother."

"You didn't think she would be?" Rory asked.

"No, *I* knew… Alexa was the one who doubted it. It will be good for her to spend some time with Kyle."

"Good for Alexa?" she echoed. "Because she's worried about motherhood?"

"Well, yeah."

Too late, Chance turned his attention back to Rory. He didn't know what he'd done to make his sister's eyes narrow like that, but nothing good could possibly come of it.

"Hey, girls, my big brother just had a brilliant idea," she announced as she reached for the baby's bag. "He's volunteered to watch Kyle while we go out to lunch."

"Wait! What?" Pure reflex had Chance catching the diaper bag that hit him straight in the chest—right along with a huge dose of panic. "No!"

Chapter Twelve

"Are you sure Kyle's going to be okay?" Alexa asked as the four of them sat down at one of the white wrought-iron tables inside the Sugar & Spice café. The small space was sunny and cheerful, with buttery yellow walls, white wainscot and primary-colored accents in the ceramic pots of fresh herbs displayed on floating shelves.

The scent of vanilla and cinnamon filled the air and gorgeously crafted desserts glistened behind a gleaming glass display, but Alexa was too distracted by thoughts of the man—and baby—they'd left behind.

"My three brothers have all taken turns watching Kyle, and only one of them has experience with babies, and that was over a decade ago. If Kyle can survive the Pirelli brothers, he can survive Chance."

"Personally, I'm more worried about my big brother than I am about Kyle. Did you see the look on his face when I *suggested* he babysit?"

Pretending to fan herself with a laminated menu, Sophia said, "I'd rather talk about the look on Chance's face when he first came charging over. He looked like he was ready to rescue Alexa from fire-breathing dragons."

"Hey, I think I resent that," Rory interjected.

Wishing she could fan her own suddenly heated face without drawing too much attention to herself, Alexa shook her head. "I'm sure Chance was just worried about the baby."

"I've seen a worried-about-the-baby look," Sophia pointed out. "That was not it. That was definitely a man-worried-about-his-woman look."

Nerves danced in Alexa's stomach, and she fisted her hands in her lap, frightened by how badly she wanted to believe the other woman might be right. That the caring and concern Chance had shown over the past few days was more than a sense of responsibility for the child she carried.

Had he given her just a hint that his feelings for her were because of something more than overwhelming attraction or the *result* of that attraction when he proposed, Alexa was afraid she very well might have said yes.

"Stop, Sophia," Lindsay chided gently. "At least allow Alexa some chocolate reinforcement before you start investigating."

"Oh, all right," the brunette agreed. "But you are having dessert first, aren't you?"

Alexa couldn't help but laugh, though she was relieved when the dark-eyed woman's attention shifted to the server who stopped by to take their order. And, no, Alexa did not order dessert first, settling instead for a grilled turkey panini with a garden salad for a side.

As the server walked away, Lindsay leaned forward,

her eyes bright with excitement as she said, "I'm so glad everything for the shower is coming together."

At Alexa's questioning glance, Rory explained. "Lindsay's sister-in-law, Nina, is due right before Christmas, and we're having the shower at Hillcrest."

"And we can't thank you enough for offering to let us use the parlor room, not to mention asking Chance to take pictures."

Rory waved aside the thanks. "Hey, as long as he's here, I'm planning to put him to work."

As long as he was there.

Alexa's appetite faded as worry about the future grabbed hold. She had promised Chance she would stay through the end of the month before heading back to LA. But she had no idea where Chance's next assignment might take him.

"Nina's going to be so surprised. It's her third baby," Lindsay was saying, "so she said she didn't want a shower."

"But we couldn't let that happen."

"Absolutely not. A baby is always something to celebrate." Seeming to have read into all Alexa hadn't said earlier, Rory repeated, "Always."

As the server arrived with their food, Alexa forced herself to focus on the positive. "Thank you again for inviting me. This looks wonderful, and it's nice to get out." Alexa cut herself off before she could add "with friends." That would be assuming too much, and while neither Sophia nor Lindsay questioned her tagging along, Alexa hadn't missed the whispered conversation between brother and sister. She was certain Chance had had something to do with his sister's sudden invitation.

"Of course. And, Lindsay, you and Alexa have something in common," Rory told the blond-haired woman as she added a splash of vinaigrette to her salad. "She's in charge of fund-raising for the Mayhew Foundation, her grandmother's charity organization."

Turning to Alexa, Rory added, "Lindsay works for the chamber of commerce, and she just organized a rodeo benefit for a local horse rescue a few months ago."

Lindsay shook her head. "Jarrett Deeks and his wife, Theresa—who also happens to be Sophia's cousin—did the majority of the legwork. I mostly helped with the advertising and reaching out for donations. Still, I was happy that the rodeo was such a success. And the best part is that they've already been able to make some upgrades to the stalls and take on more horses with the money raised."

"How wonderful that you can see the good your work has done firsthand."

"Well," Lindsay said, her cheeks brightening at the praise, "it's nothing on scale to all you've accomplished."

The foundation had raised millions of dollars over the years, but rarely did Alexa see that money put into use. She talked to people who knew people, and made sure the events went off without a hitch. And then at the end of the night, she would present the head of the charity with a big check—literally—as she smiled and posed for pictures.

But then she would move on. To the next charity in need and to the next celebrity golf tournament, star-studded concert or golden gala. The foundation received pictures of improved schools or health clinics or housing for those in need. But that wasn't the same as seeing the benefits firsthand.

"I've actually been considering taking on a different role at the foundation," Alexa said, speaking her thoughts out loud for the first time to an audience who didn't know her well enough to judge. Who wouldn't limit her possibilities with all a Mayhew did not do. "I'd like to be more hands-on and work with the charities to come up with financial plans for how to best use the funds raised. Finding a way to maintain donor interest in those projects might help the public realize charities don't just need money during fund-raising drives or at the holidays."

Embarrassed by her own unexpected outpouring, Alexa cut herself off and reached for her glass of water. "Sorry, I'm probably getting a little far ahead of myself."

But Lindsay only shook her head. "That sounds like a really good idea. In fact, I'd love to do some brainstorming with you while you're here. That is if you don't mind."

"And I can set up something with Jarrett and Theresa if you want to take a look around their rescue and see what they've accomplished so far," Sophia offered.

"I wouldn't mind at all," Alexa said, surprised and pleased by how readily the other women had embraced her ideas. Starting out small would be a great way to get her feet wet as well as an opportunity to give back to the small town she was coming to love.

The sound of a muffled ringtone had Sophia pushing back from the table. "Oh, excuse me for a second," she said as she dropped her napkin on the chair and answered her cell.

The three women talked a bit more about Lindsay's position at the chamber of commerce as well as the town's areas of need before Sophia returned to the table. "Sorry about that. Jake, my husband, has been out of town. I thought he'd be back tonight, but he's been delayed."

"Is everything okay?" Lindsay asked.

"He has assured me 'not to worry.' Which means that's all I'll be doing until I hear from him again."

"What does your husband do?" Alexa asked, recalling what the other woman had said earlier about her husband's frequent travels.

"He's a private investigator."

The unexpected answer had Alexa setting her sandwich aside. "Wow. That sounds interesting."

"Jake swears it's not, and that ninety percent of the time, it's totally boring. It's that ten percent that keeps me up at night."

"I don't imagine it's much like they show on television."

"Don't even get him started on those comparisons! Although my brothers love to tease him. For his last birthday, they all bought him Hawaiian shirts in tribute to *Magnum, P.I.* You know, that popular detective show from the eighties? Believe me when I tell you Jake is not a Hawaiian shirt kind of guy."

"Still, it must be hard when he's gone." Alexa tried to imagine her son or daughter calling a man other than Chance "da-da" and didn't think she'd handle it nearly as well as Sophia had.

"It is." The brunette's smile trembled a bit, revealing that it wasn't as easy as she made it seem. "But I have friends and family to help out, and I know he misses me as much as I miss him. But this is more than a job to Jake. It's so much a part of him that I can't imagine him doing anything else." Her dark eyes brimmed with emotion as she added, "His love for me has always been completely and irrevocably unconditional. How can I possibly deserve that unless my love for him is the same?"

Though Chance was sure Rory thought otherwise, he did occasionally listen to his sister. And when he did, more often than not, he was forced to admit she was right. Which probably accounted for why he didn't listen more often.

He hated admitting she was right. He especially hadn't liked it when she'd pointed out how lacking his proposal to Alexa had been.

Were there flowers? Music? A ring? Didn't you see

Alexa at the reception, willing to dance with perfect strangers just to make them smile? This is a woman who's looking for romance and longing for a man to sweep her off her feet.

Alexa deserved all of that and more, but other than that first weekend together, he'd shown her very little of it. Something he was trying to make up for as he led Alexa down the gravel path from the cottage.

"Are you sure your eyes are closed?"

"I'm sure, although why they are closed, I don't know," Alexa said, her hands to her face. "Is this some kind of payback for leaving you to babysit Kyle?"

"You do know what they say about revenge being sweet," he teased. He did still owe Rory for that whole bait and switch she'd pulled the other day. "I cannot tell you how much energy that kid has."

After two hours, he'd been exhausted and overwhelmed—but so excited to meet his own kid, he didn't know how he was going to wait another five months.

Of course, he couldn't blame Alexa if she wasn't quite so eager. He'd seen the look on her face when she'd walked into the cottage. Every toy, every piece of clothing, every diaper had been tossed out of the oversize diaper bag. Kyle had had a field day playing with all of it—but none of it for more than fifteen seconds at a time.

From there, he'd moved on to a stuffed bear left over from Rory's childhood. A perfectly suitable plaything, Chance had thought, until the little boy pulled off one of the bear's button eyes and popped it into his mouth. Panicked, Chance had scooped up the baby, holding him upside down until he spit out the button much to the little boy's dismay.

Figuring if the kid was hungry enough to eat inedible objects, lunch ought to be a piece of cake. After a scene

involving pureed peas that would have done the special
effects artist from *The Exorcist* proud, the cottage was
soon littered with the majority of Chance's wardrobe as
he'd had to change his shirt. Three times. By the end of
the meal, both he and Kyle were half-naked. The little boy
keeping on his long-sleeved T-shirt, diaper and one sock
while Chance settled on wearing just his jeans.

Finally, after having been sufficiently worn out, Kyle
had settled down in Chance's arms for a nap. Which was
where Alexa had found them an hour or so later.

Alexa, he had to admit, had been a trooper. She'd helped
him redress Kyle, pack up his numerous belongings and
return him to his mother—more or less in the same shape
as when she'd left him.

"Poor baby," she commiserated now.

"Me or the kid?"

"Oh, you. Definitely you."

"I just hope Kyle didn't end up eating his other shoe.
I'm telling you, I have no idea where that thing went."

"I have a feeling it will turn up somewhere."

"Okay, we're here." Positioning Alexa for the best vantage point for his surprise, he said, "You can open your
eyes."

Dropping her hands, she let out a gasp as she caught
her first glimpse of the gazebo. A table draped in white
sat in the middle of the platform. Covered dishes gleamed
in the twinkle lights draped overhead, and colorful pots of
burgundy, orange and yellow mums lined the steps along
with garland draped on either side of the stair railings.
"Oh, Chance. How beautiful!"

"I thought after the busy day we've both had, that a nice
quiet dinner would be just what we needed."

A nice *romantic* dinner, he could almost hear Rory
whispering in his ear.

He'd bungled his proposal to Alexa. Badly. While he might not be ready to put his heart on the line, Alexa was a woman who deserved candlelight dinners, wine—or for now sparkling cider—and flowers.

"We've kind of gone about this all backward," he admitted as he guided her up the steps. "To say we rushed things in Santa Barbara might be a bit of an understatement."

"You think?" she teased, the candlelight reflected in her eyes as she sank into the chair he pulled out for her.

"And I certainly rushed that proposal the other night, so I was thinking that maybe we could not start over, but just a few steps back and take things a bit slower this time."

Her lashes lowered as she ducked her head almost shyly. "I think I'd like that." And then dispelling any sense of shyness as well as most of the thoughts from his head, she added, "Although I was looking forward to another cooking lesson for dinner."

"Well, there's always breakfast in the morning." Which left so many possibilities open for tonight.

All of which would once again fall into the "rushing things" category.

"Are you warm enough?" Chance asked sometime after they had finished the mouthwatering meal from the hotel restaurant. He had to hand it to Evie, who'd somehow convinced the up-and-coming chef to leave San Francisco to come work at Hillcrest. The man had outdone himself with roasted Cornish game hens, sautéed asparagus and brown sugar sweet potatoes.

Alexa had wanted a better view of the stars while they ate their dessert, so Chance had switched off the lights and carried the plate over to where she'd taken a seat on the stairs. She had her arms wrapped around her knees, and although he had warned her to dress warmly and brought two propane heaters out for the occasion, he wanted to make sure she was comfortable.

"I'm fine," she reassured him as he sat down beside her.

He wrapped an arm around her shoulders—just to be safe—and felt something sweet and powerful settle into his chest as she rested her head against his shoulder.

"Mm, pumpkin cheesecake," Alexa almost groaned as he offered her the dessert, the sound sending a burst of heat straight to his gut. And when she closed her lips around the fork, it was all he could do to form a coherent sentence.

"Evie's all about offering guests a seasonal menu."

"Everything was wonderful."

"Not bad for a first date?"

She laughed a little at that. "Not bad at all."

They sat in a comfortable silence as she dug into the crumbly graham cracker crust. She had just set the plate aside when she pointed to a streak across the night sky. "Oh, look! A shooting star…" She sucked in a breath, and though the movement was slight, Chance felt her pull away. Her shoulders slumped as she drew her legs up onto the next step, curling into herself as if trying to shield her heart.

He tightened his arm around her, an instinctive urge to protect her from anything, everything, rising inside him. "Alexa? What's wrong?"

"That's what my grandmother sometimes called my parents. Shooting stars."

"Do you want to tell me about them?"

"They were like Christmas and New Year's and the Fourth of July—fun and exciting."

And only came around a few times a year. Alexa didn't say the words, but he heard them in the wistfulness in her voice. His heart broke a little as the moonlight touched on the sad smile on her beautiful face. Reaching over with his free hand, he threaded his fingers through hers and squeezed. "I'm sorry, sweetheart."

"It was a long time ago. Twenty years ago." Her shoulders straightened slightly as she turned to face him. "The day you called was—that was the anniversary of my parents' death, Chance."

"Oh, Lexi…"

"I spent the first half of my childhood waiting for them to call, to come home. I saw myself falling into that same pattern with you, and I didn't want to be that little girl again."

"And so you told me it was over."

"Yes." That abrupt conversation still stung, but Chance felt he understood better now. "I'm sorry…"

"I don't want to hear that you're sorry. I want to hear that it's not true." Chance heard the touch of desperation in his own voice and forced his grip on her slender hand to relax. "That maybe that weekend meant more than a meaningless fling…"

"It meant…enough to scare me. To leave me feeling vulnerable."

"Just like that phone call left me feeling. All that talk about different lives. I saw you that night at the hotel, surrounded by some of the wealthiest people in California, and there I was—a high school dropout who's spent most of his adult life living out of a beat-up backpack, thinking to myself, 'What the hell am I doing here?'"

"But that—that's not what I meant!" It was her turn to tighten her grip, the skin-to-skin communication mattering as much as the words. "Not at all! Chance, you're talented, successful, famous! That's why you were invited to that benefit. That's why half the people were in attendance, to meet you!"

He gave a rough chuckle. "I'd say half is a definite exaggeration. But the point is, you belonged there, and I didn't."

"You're so confident, so at ease in your own skin, I honestly can't imagine a place where you wouldn't belong."

It had suited him well over the years, his ability to adapt, to fit in. But Chance wasn't sure he'd ever felt as truly comfortable, as completely in the present as he had with Alexa by his side. He wasn't working an angle, wasn't digging deeper to uncover some hidden truth. He'd allowed himself to simply enjoy the moment, to accept the chemistry and connection for what it was.

"The only time I felt like I belonged that night was when I held you in my arms." Alexa glowed in the soft moonlight, but Chance still saw the shadows from a childhood where she'd been so easily left behind. "I wanted to carry that feeling, to carry a piece of you with me, Alexa. That's why I didn't give the butterfly hairpin back."

"So you had it with you...the whole time?"

"The whole time," he echoed. It had become his touchstone, a good memory to combat all the bad.

"And you still think it's lucky?"

"I know it is," he said, thinking back to the day when the small memento had saved his life.

He'd been moments away from stepping inside a building to interview an outspoken political dissident. After paying off the guide who had led him to the meeting place, Chance had stuck his hand back into his pocket. His fingers had brushed against the butterfly, and in an instant he'd been taken back to that weekend. Back to Alexa.

His head hadn't been anywhere near where it should have been—preparing for the interview—something that in another place or time might have gotten him killed. But in that moment, with Alexa filling his thoughts, he'd taken an extra moment to refocus. He'd waited outside a minute. Maybe two. But long enough that when the building some twenty feet from him exploded, he was far enough away to survive.

He had Alexa to thank for that, but the story wasn't one he planned to share with her. Not now. Not ever.

But almost as if reading his thoughts, she asked, "Can—can I ask you about your work? If you don't want to talk about it—"

"No, it's okay. What do you want to know?" But even as he asked the question, he braced himself. His job had always been a sore spot. First with his parents and later with Lisette.

"When did you first realize you wanted to be a photographer?"

The easy question caught him off guard, and he felt himself relax. "When I was still a teenager, not too long after my dad gave me one of his old 35 millimeter cameras."

"Your dad?"

"He's a photographer, too."

Alexa was silent for a moment before she said, "I noticed some tension between the two of you. At first I thought it was about the baby, but it was there even before you made your announcement."

"It isn't you, Alexa, or the baby. It's me. It's always been me. I'm—I'm not who my parents want me to be."

"What does that mean?"

"They love me, I know that, and I love them. And if I was a different person—maybe a better person—then maybe I could change. Maybe I could put aside my own dreams and do what they want me to do. But ask anyone. I'm selfish. Always thinking of myself first and my family second. Or to hear my father tell it, not thinking of them at all."

Not thinking of Alexa or the baby at all. That was what his father had said after pulling him aside in the final moments before they drove off. And that accusation hurt more than Chance wanted to admit. Because his father thought so little of him? Or because deep down, he couldn't help wondering if the words were true.

"What do they want you to be?"

"When I was a kid, I was always the wild child. The one who thought the word *no* simply meant I should do what I want without getting caught." He gave a short laugh. "Only I almost always got caught—doing stupid stuff, mostly. There wasn't a dare I could back down from or a chance I wouldn't take even as a little kid."

"So you were…you. Even then."

"Yeah, I guess that's one way of looking at it. I thought I was invincible until I was twelve or so and found I wasn't as hardheaded as everyone thought."

"What happened?"

"I was messing around on a skateboard. Trying a trick on a half-pipe that I was nowhere near skilled enough to complete. I landed wrong, hit my head and…ended up in a coma."

"Oh, my God!"

Chance heard the shock, the concern in Alexa's voice. Just a fraction of the emotion that his parents must have felt, but as for Chance, he didn't remember the accident or the weeks and months that followed. He hadn't understood how he could wake up one day only to discover everything had changed.

"I fully recovered, but in a way, I'm not sure my parents ever did. Not completely. After the accident, they couldn't protect me enough. For the longest time, they didn't even want me out of their sight."

"And you hated that."

"Hated it, rebelled against it. Fought even harder to do whatever I wanted, whenever I wanted. And then when I was fourteen or so, I started to get interested in photography. At first they were all for it. I think they hoped if I channeled all my energy into photography, I'd be happy taking pictures of, I don't know, kittens and puppies. But I was still me. I still wanted to be out hiking and climbing and biking—only with a camera in hand.

"After high school, my parents wanted me to go to college and work part-time at my dad's studio. Taking family photos, graduation shots, baby pictures." Even after all that time, just thinking about being trapped in that small studio—both physically and creatively *stuck*—was enough to make Chance want to take off at a dead run. "Instead I took off for LA, and I never looked back."

"And you have an incredible career. You can't tell me your parents aren't proud of the man—the photojournalist—you've become."

"I always thought so until this happened," he said, stretching out his right leg and still feeling the reminders of the damage done by the explosion in the strain in the joint and muscles. "Until I woke up in the hospital after my last surgery and overheard my parents talking about how it might be better if I never fully regained use of my leg again."

"Oh, Chance…"

Just saying the words out loud, he was taken back to that moment. To the sterile white walls, the beeping of the machines, the sharp, antiseptic smell of the recovery room. His parents hadn't realized he was awake, and in truth, he hadn't been. Drifting in and out of consciousness, but aware of enough to know he hadn't misunderstood any of what he heard.

"This is my life, the career I've always wanted. The one

I dreamed about since I was a kid and that they would actually be *glad* if I were injured badly enough to have to give it up…" His throat burned, searing all the way down as he swallowed the words he couldn't bring himself to say.

"Chance, they're your parents." Her gentle blue-gray gaze pleaded with him as she said, "They love you—"

"Love," he bit out roughly. "If that's love, I don't want any part of it."

Chapter Thirteen

If that's love, I don't want any part of it.

At the bitterness slicing through Chance's voice and straight to her heart, Alexa could have cried. Not for herself, but for him. Beneath the anger, the rejection, she heard the pain. How often as a child had she wondered what more she could have done? If only she'd been smarter, funnier, more interesting, then maybe her parents would have stayed. Maybe they would have lived.

The situation wasn't exactly the same. Her parents hadn't loved her enough to stay. Chance's parents loved him too much to let him go. But too much or not enough, that love wasn't *unconditional*.

She couldn't deny that she understood the fear and the longing in his parents' desire to keep their son safe. As much as she admired his talent, his courage, his convictions, she hated the thought of him putting his life in danger.

She'd already felt a fraction of what it would be like to

lose him when she heard the news reports. But that was before she'd truly gotten to know him beyond the sexy, confident man she'd had such an entirely out-of-character fling with. She'd seen his moments of doubt and vulnerability, how the horrors of what he'd witnessed through his lens haunted him. She'd seen him completely in over his head with little Kyle and loving every minute of it.

She'd seen the kind of man—the kind of husband, the kind of father—he could be, and she didn't know how to protect herself from that Chance McClaren.

But then she thought of their weekend together. How being with Chance had made her feel reckless, wild and unafraid. If making love had made her brave enough to take a chance for a weekend, was it possible that loving him with her whole heart might make her strong enough to take a chance on the love of a lifetime?

He pushed away from the steps, his long strides carrying him a few yards before he stopped short. His tall, broad-shouldered form was little more than a shadowed silhouette, but tension radiated from his unnatural stillness. Alexa sensed the slightest movement might send him running. She had an idea of what might make him stay if she had the courage to be the woman she was always meant to be.

"It's getting cold," he said abruptly. "I'll walk you back to the cottage."

Slowly lowering her feet to the ground, she stood and walked over to his side. She ran a hand down his arm, waiting until his muscles relaxed to link her fingers with his. They were silent on the walk back, but the slow pace did little to ease the raw energy building inside him.

Though she had given in to his insistence that she sleep in the bedroom, the cottage was small. The thin wall between them did little to block out the sound of his restless nights, and he was always gone in the morning when she woke. More than once she'd slipped from the bed in the middle of the night to stand by the door, afraid to turn the knob. Knowing if she did, she wouldn't have been inviting Chance into the bedroom, but into her heart.

He stopped on the porch when she tried to draw him inside. "I'm going to go clean up the gazebo. I'll be back later."

Her heart pounding, Alexa swallowed. "Chance?"

He half turned back to her as if caught in a moment of indecision. Stay…or go?

"You asked me my first morning here how I slept the night before. I lied. The truth is, I haven't had a good night's sleep since the last time you were in my bed." Holding his gaze as she repeated him word for word, she added, "I can't close my eyes without imagining you there."

His eyes widened, and this time when he ran, it was back to her. His long strides ate up the distance, his limp almost imperceptible, and her heart trembled a little at what that would mean in the near future. But she didn't want to think about that now. And then Chance kissed her, and she didn't want to think about anything. Not the past or the future. Nothing but the swirling, impatient passion of the present.

She wrapped her arms around his shoulders and held him tight as he backed her toward the cottage. The solid muscle contrasted with the soft cotton shirt, and she couldn't get enough, would never get enough.

He fumbled with the doorknob as if not wanting to let her go for more than a second, and she wasn't sure how they made it to the bedroom. By the time they crossed the threshold, she had already stripped off his shirt, laying claim to the smooth skin of his shoulders and his hair-roughened chest.

He helped pull her sweater over her head, the skirt down her hips, and then he froze. A split second of uncertainty washed over Alexa, leaving her feeling, well, exposed in nothing but her black lace bra and panties. But then she realized what had captured his attention as his gaze locked on the swell of her belly, the low-cut lace flaunting the roundness.

A brief hesitation held them both spellbound. And then Chance stroked his fingers over her stomach. Her muscles trembled at the light touch, but it was the look of amazement that shook her to her soul. "Chance…" Her voice broke, and Alexa knew her heart might soon follow, but she had no choice. She was falling in love with him.

He swallowed hard and then lifted his gaze to hers. "Alexa, I have a confession to make…" Despite the weighted moment and the seriousness of his words, a teasing light entered his eyes. "You're not gonna get a good night sleep with me in your bed tonight."

"Something tells me you'll make it up to me. And besides," she said with a tempting, tender smile as she pressed his palm to her belly and their baby, "it's not like you can get me more pregnant."

His eyes glowed as he lowered his head and brushed his mouth across hers. Alexa reveled in a hint of the dessert that tasted a hundred times richer on his lips than it had on the fork.

But unlike a sweet tooth, which could be sated, every kiss made Alexa's hunger grow. She was dizzy and aching by the time Chance brushed aside the bit of lace undergarments, then stepped away to strip off the rest of his clothes. Eager to be back in his embrace, she threw her arms around his broad shoulders as he lowered her to the bed.

Bracing his weight above her, he asked, "Is this…okay?"

His caring and concern touched her heart as thoroughly and powerfully as his caresses touched her body. "More than okay," she reassured him with a breathless gasp. "It's perfect."

When he lowered himself between her thighs, thrusting inside, she felt whole. And when he took her in his arms, it was like coming home. Chance rocked against her, each shallow thrust striking sparks of desire inside and out. Pleasure spiraled out of control, cresting and breaking. Alexa clung to him, wrapping her limbs around him as he shuddered and rode his own wave of release.

Gradually the rhythm rippling their bodies slowed, then stopped, but still Alexa refused to let go, wanting the moment to last. Wanting to hold on tight…and to never have to let go.

Years ago, Chance had brought Lisette home to Medford to meet his family. She'd acted as though his hometown and the entire state of Oregon, for that matter, was some kind of untamed wilderness. He could only imagine how she would have dismissed the tiny, quaint town of Clearville in a single glance.

Only a few weeks ago, he would have thought Alexa might do the same, but the more time they spent together, the more he realized how different she was from his ex. In a short amount of time, she'd already become a part of his sister's inner circle of friends. Sharing ideas with Rory on decorating the hotel for the upcoming holidays. Meeting with Lindsay to discuss events planned by the chamber of commerce. Planning to talk with Theresa and Jarrett Deeks about fund-raising ideas for the couple's horse rescue.

Hell, she fit in better than he did.

From the orchard where visitors could pick their own apples, to the horse-drawn carriage rides through town, to the dozens of tiny shops along Main Street, she lived it all with a wide-eyed enjoyment that grabbed hold of his heart and wouldn't let go.

Showing her around the town brought back memories of how much he loved coming to Clearville as a kid. The hours he'd spent exploring everything from the rugged coastline to the towering redwoods to the acres of farmland. And now, seeing it all again as an adult with a photographer's eye...

"I told you," Alexa had said at one point as they walked along the beach, her blue-gray eyes laughing at him as she lifted a hand to keep her blond hair from blowing in the ocean breeze. She wore a cream-colored sweater over a pale-blue-and-white-striped dress, the soft material molding to the curves of her breasts and the curve of their baby.

"What?"

"That you should have brought your camera with you. You're dying to capture all of this. Your index finger has been twitching all afternoon," she teased.

"It has not," he argued, even though she was right. Though he'd never given serious thought to nature photography, with such vast and varied landscapes all around him, it was almost impossible not to try to line up the perfect shot in his mind's eye.

But he'd refused to bring his camera.

Something was happening to him here. Something about his time in Clearville was softening his focus, changing the angle of his lens.

What had Alexa said when looking through the wedding pictures he'd taken?

Seeing these pictures makes me feel like I'm seeing the real you.

For so long he'd narrowed his gaze on the turbulent moments of life and human nature. Capturing a darkness too many people wanted to turn a blind eye to. His work was important, yet after such a short time around his family, around Alexa, he could feel himself losing his edge. He was relaxing, breathing easier, slowing down.

All fine and good for recovering from his injuries. But that kind of lax attitude could get him killed in the field. He couldn't just expect to pick up his guard along with his camera before heading out to the next job.

Over the past half decade, he'd traveled an average of nine months out of the year. The grueling schedule was starting to pay off. His articles were gaining recognition; he was being offered more and more choice assignments. Could he really walk away from his career just as he was nearing the pinnacle he'd strived to reach for so long?

He didn't have an answer to that question, and he was running out of time. His leg was getting stronger every day. His editor was expecting him to be on a plane by the end of the month to take an assignment he hadn't told Alexa about yet. And Alexa was expecting—

Alexa was expecting his child and, he feared, more than he knew how to give.

Stepping closer, he watched her eyes widen with sensual awareness as he bent his head toward hers. "There's something else I want to capture, and I'd rather not have a camera in my hands while I do this…"

He pulled her into his arms and kissed her then, the salt from the ocean air and pure seduction of her lips beneath her own wiping away any thoughts of leaving. "Or this…"

Alexa's startled laugh turned into a playful scream as he scooped her up into his arms and charged toward the frigid surf.

"Thank you again for inviting me out to the ranch," Alexa told Theresa Deeks as the two of them stood outside a corral, watching as Jarrett worked with one of the Rockin' R's horses.

Along with running the horse rescue, the Deekses offered rental cabins for tourists and visitors who wanted to stay outside of town. From what she could see, they had picked a prime location. Towering redwoods lined the surrounding acres, climbing toward the clouds overhead and extending to the mountains in the distance. A sense of peace filled the property, with the rustle of the wind in the trees and the whinny of a horse the only sounds.

Alexa wished she could grab hold of some of that peace for herself. The past few days with Chance had been some of the happiest of her life. She loved walking down Main Street with him, strolling through the Victorian shops the town was known for; holding his hand while they explored the grounds around Hillcrest; soaking up the sounds of the ocean as they combed the beach for seashells.

And the nights…she had no doubt about how much he wanted her when they made love or even in the quiet moments after when he would reach for her in his sleep.

On the outside, everything was…perfect. But beneath the surface, she sensed something was wrong. Little ripples of unease that she worried hid turbulent water below. Like that morning when she'd asked him to come to the ranch with her. Confidence had filled his sexy smile as he kissed her. "You've got this, Alexa. You don't need me."

Maybe she didn't *need* him, but she wanted him to be with her…and she was very much afraid he already wanted to be somewhere else.

"I should be thanking you," Theresa was saying. "The rodeo benefit was a first for us, and we're thrilled with the results. The donations and the percentage of the take from the ticket sales were more than what we hoped for, but then trying to come up with the best way to use that money…"

She shook her head, her dark ponytail swinging back and forth. "You wouldn't think that would be a problem, but deciding how to spend the money was almost as daunting as not having the money to spend."

Refocusing on her reason for going out to the ranch, Alexa said, "It's always hard especially for a smaller rescue operation like the one you and Jarrett run here. Trying to figure out where your greatest need is, well, it's like triage," Alexa said. As a nurse, Theresa would be very familiar with the concept.

"That's exactly what it is," Theresa said, her eyes lighting in realization as the two of them walked back to the stables. "I can't believe I never thought of it that way, but with the financial plan you came up with, I feel like I have a better handle on where to go from here. And I love the idea of an open house."

In the past few months since the benefit, Jarrett and Theresa had already put some of the money raised to good use, making improvements to the stables, stocking up on feed and taking in more horses. "You've made some amazing changes already," Alexa said. "From the way you described it, most of Clearville turned out for the rodeo. I'm sure people would love to see how you've put their donations to use, and it's important to keep the rescue in the public eye. I know you're hoping to make the rodeo an annual event, but you can't rely on one fund-raiser to support the rescue for an entire year."

As Theresa led the way into the stables, the two of them discussed contacting local businesses to see who might be willing to volunteer or donate food, entertainment and advertising for the event. Alexa figured the ranch and the horses themselves would be a huge draw. The sights and sounds of the stables were as unfamiliar as the rich, earthy scents of hay and horses, but she was fascinated by the beautiful animals eyeing her curiously from their stalls.

"I don't believe my eyes!"

Startled by the sound of a feminine voice, Alexa turned to see a blonde smiling her delight as she walked down the concrete aisle between the stalls. "I swear that is the first designer outfit I have seen in the six months since I moved here!"

Not completely unprepared for the trip out to the Rockin' R, Alexa had worn boots. But the black suede pair she'd matched with her black, wide-legged trousers and emerald green ribbed turtleneck sweater were nothing like Theresa's or this woman's sturdy, well-worn footwear.

She couldn't help but smile, though, at the other woman's enthusiasm. "Well, you seemed to have survived despite the lack of high-end fashion."

"Never let it be said I can't rock a pair of Wranglers," she said with a full turn that would have done a model on a catwalk proud. Sighing as she ran her palms down the untucked red-and-black flannel shirt. "But I do miss the opportunity to dress up more often."

"You have to excuse my sister-in-law. She's still adjusting to life in a small town where you buy clothes at the same place where you pick up your groceries," Theresa said with a smile at the younger woman.

Alexa hoped she managed to hide her surprise. She'd been charmed by Jarrett Deeks's soft-spoken Midwestern drawl, as well as with his obvious devotion to his dark-haired wife. She wouldn't have imagined that this petite blonde with corkscrew curls and outspoken sass would be related to him.

"Summer, this is Alexa Mayhew. She's a friend of Rory McClaren's."

Summer's cornflower blue eyes widened. "Oh, my

gosh! Do you know Chance McClaren? I am one of his biggest fans. I keep hoping I'll run into him in town, but so far, no luck."

Alexa didn't want to feel jealous that this beautiful, wide-eyed woman wanted the chance to meet her idol. Didn't want to think of the adoring fans he had around the world.

As Summer went on about the color and composition of his photos, Alexa realized the other woman hadn't exaggerated about being a true fan—and not simply of Chance as a handsome, successful photojournalist, but of his photographs.

Jarrett called his sister's name from the doorway to the stables, and the bubbly blonde headed out to give a riding lesson, but not before asking if Alexa would introduce her to Chance.

"Sorry about that," Theresa said as she led the way into the small office in the corner of the stables. "Summer can be a bit exuberant at times, but that's why we love her. And while I'll admit I'm a little biased, she truly is a talented photographer. She's taken all of the pictures for the rescue's website and for our Home, Sweet Home wall."

Theresa waved a hand to the space behind the desk and the collage of horses posing with their adoptive families. But it was another picture that caught Alexa's eye. One of a denim-and-flannel-dressed cowboy hovering midair above a ferocious black bull. "Is that Jarrett?"

"That it is," Theresa confirmed. "Back in his bull riding days."

After watching the cowboy in the corral for only a few moments, Alexa had seen his quiet confidence and skill with the horses, but this—this was something else. "Isn't that...dangerous?"

"That it is," the brunette repeated. "Fortunately, that

was back in the days before we met. Before a pretty serious injury put an end to his rodeo career."

"What would you do," Alexa asked, her pulse suddenly pounding in her ears, "if that injury healed to the point where Jarrett wanted to ride again?"

Theresa exhaled a breath. "Boy, I've never really thought about that before." Leaning back against the edge of the desk, she said, "I didn't know Jarrett when he was competing, but I have an idea of how important it was to him, how much he loved it. Giving it up was hard on him, and if he hadn't turned his attention to rescuing horses, I hate to think of the darker paths he might have chosen. So, even though I know how dangerous bull riding can be, even though a part of me would always, well, hate it, to be perfectly honest, I'd have to do all I could to support him.

"Maybe my own career as a trauma nurse gives me a different perspective. I know how quickly life can change. From illness, to injuries, to accidents, you never know what might happen, no matter how careful you are. For me, it was a car accident."

"Were you seriously injured?"

"Seriously enough," Theresa admitted. "When I first came here, I was still hurting. I honestly didn't know if I would recover to the point where I could go back to the job I loved, and Jarrett was there for me. He had a faith in me that I didn't have in myself."

"But that's not the same thing, is it? Nursing doesn't come with the dangers of being a photo…I mean, bull rider," Alexa amended at the last second.

Theresa's knowing smile acknowledged the slip, but she merely said, "True. But at the time, going back to work meant going back to St. Louis. His life was here and mine, I thought, was there. So, as clichéd as it might sound, Jarrett loved me enough to let me go, which in the end is what gave me the strength to stay."

Letting go of someone she loved… Alexa felt she'd lived her whole life letting go. Could she find a way to hold on to the hope that she might be reason enough for Chance to stay?

Chapter Fourteen

"Are you ready for this?" Chance asked as he pulled into a parking space and cut the engine.

Sucking in a deep breath, Alexa gazed at the three-story building in front of them. "I didn't expect to be so nervous," she admitted, her hands tightening on the seat belt without releasing the latch.

After the tour of the Rockin' R ranch, Theresa had invited Alexa to stay for lunch. Over sandwiches piled high with shaved roast beef, lettuce and tomato, the other woman had asked about Alexa's pregnancy. Before she knew it, Alexa was sharing more personal details than she ever would have expected to with a perfect stranger. But Theresa's compassion and calm demeanor made her easy to talk to.

Maybe it was all part of the pretty nurse's bedside manner even though they'd both been sitting at the kitchen table at the time.

And when Alexa admitted she'd had to cancel her ultrasound appointment back home after her stay in Clearville had lasted longer than planned, Theresa had recommended an obstetrician at the medical clinic in nearby Redfield.

"Will they be able to tell if it's a boy or a girl?" Chance asked.

"Possibly, if the baby cooperates and is in the right position. Do you want to know what we're having?"

"I'm not sure. I think…I'd rather be surprised. To find out in that moment when we first meet our child whether we have a son or a daughter."

In that moment…

After pulling the key from the ignition, Chance climbed from the SUV, but Alexa couldn't bring herself to move as he rounded the hood to open her door.

His eyebrows rose when he realized she was still buckled into her seat. Concern filled his expression as he crouched by her side. "Hey, everything okay? You're not that worried about the scan, are you?"

"No, I'm fine." Alexa shook her head, and she unbuckled her seat belt and grabbed her purse. Her hands trembled as she held tight to the leather strap. Not with fear, but with the faint stirrings of hope. She'd been steeling herself from the beginning to face going through labor alone.

But now, with Chance making it sound as though he wanted to be in the delivery room with her, she pressed a hand to her trembling stomach. She wanted him there. She *desperately* wanted him to be there, but if she started to count on that, to count on him, and if he let her down…

Whenever his cell phone rang and he stepped out of the room to take the call, her heart practically leaped from her chest. Each time, she waited for him to tell her he was taking another assignment, biting her lip to keep from begging him not to go. So far her fears had been unfounded as Chance would slip the phone back into his pocket without saying a word. But Alexa knew the day would come, and she wondered if he had any idea that when he left he'd be taking her heart with him.

Chance was silent as they headed toward the clinic's glass doors. When Alexa turned toward a large directory near the elevators, he guided her down a hall to the left.

"The obstetrician's office is this way."

Her eyebrows rose. "And you know that…how?"

"Because," he explained, "my physical therapist is a few doors down."

Which was true, but Chance had probably paid more attention to the comings and goings from the baby doctor's office than any healthy, single man should. He'd been attending therapy down the hall long enough to have seen a few hugely pregnant women arrive for an appointment one week only to return soon afterward with a newborn infant in their arms.

More than once, he'd lent a hand to a woman struggling to hold an infant in one arm while maneuvering an awkward baby carrier or enormous stroller with her free hand. And he'd wondered where their husbands, the fathers of their children were. Why were so many of the women trying to handle all this alone?

The way Alexa will be alone when you go on assignment.

Guilt tightened around his chest, making it almost impossible to breathe. The trapped, suffocating feeling was the same one he used to get on his visits home. When his mother's not-so-subtle hints about settling down and his father's more pointed comments about wanting Chance to take over the family business had sent him running.

And he'd never stopped.

For years, he'd been racing toward his goals—tracking down an elusive source, following the story wherever it led, grabbing hold of the acclaim, the awards, the highest achievements in his field.

But when he thought of leaving Alexa, of leaving their baby, he didn't feel like he was running toward his future. But more like he was running away from his past.

Heading toward the reception area, Alexa smiled at the young woman behind the desk. "I'm here for an appointment with Dr. Fitzgerald. My doctor in LA was supposed to email my records."

"Yes, Ms. Mayhew. We have them here. In looking over them, the doctor noticed some…gaps in the father's medical history?" The receptionist glanced at Chance but clearly didn't want to make any assumptions.

His jaw tightened, not as concerned about the gaps in his history as he was about the gaps in his child's future.

Embarrassment colored Alexa's cheeks as she reached for the clipboard, but Chance beat her to it. "Let's fill in some of those blanks."

The receptionist offered him a relieved smile before he and Alexa took two seats in the corner of the waiting room. Sitting ramrod straight in the chair beside him, her hands were locked around her purse strap in a death grip. "I'm sorry," she said quietly.

"Don't, Alexa. I told you before, what's done is done."

But as he filled out the forms, spelling out the details of his recent surgeries word for word, he couldn't help wondering what might have happened if Alexa had gotten ahold of him in the days before the bombing.

If he had dropped everything to go to be with her then, he might not have been injured. He would have known about her pregnancy from the start, but then what? Had he been perfectly healthy over the past three months, did he really think he would have turned down another assignment? He certainly wouldn't have come to Clearville. He wouldn't be sitting at Alexa's side now.

Without the months of recovery, time he'd spent with memories of Alexa filling his waking and sleeping hours, he might never had slowed down enough to consider a life beyond the one he'd always known.

He'd never been a big believer in fate, but… Reaching over, he grabbed Alexa's slender hand. "Some things are meant to be."

She returned his reassuring squeeze, and Chance didn't want to let go. Not even when a nurse called her name a few minutes later. The woman explained that the doctor would perform an exam first, and they would bring Chance back to the room for the ultrasound.

Finished with the forms, Chance had nothing to do but wait—and pace—while Alexa was with the doctor. He stopped abruptly when a turn by the reception desk had him nearly bumping into a very pregnant woman who had just signed in. "Sorry, I'm—"

"A first-time dad?" she guessed with a sympathetic smile.

Running a hand through his hair, he sighed. "That obvious?"

"It's been a while since we had our first, but I still recognize the signs."

Two months ago had anyone told him he would be talking babies and pregnancy with a total stranger, he would have laughed his head off. But as he helped lower the mom-to-be into one of the waiting-room chairs, he asked, "What number is this for you?"

"Our third. Another boy." She rolled her eyes. "Heaven help me." But her dreamy smile as she rested her hands on her large belly told another story.

"You look familiar." Cocking her head to one side, she said, "I know! You're Rory McClaren's brother, aren't you?

I work at a florist shop in Clearville, and we've done the flowers for some of Hillcrest's weddings."

"Oh, right." Great, now he was talking babies, flowers and weddings with a perfect stranger. He may as well forfeit his man card for all eternity. "Chance McClaren."

"I'm Nina Kincaid. It's nice to meet you."

The name rang a bell. Nina… Oh, yeah, this was Lindsay's sister-in-law and the guest of honor for the surprise baby shower at the hotel next weekend.

Did Alexa have friends in LA who would throw such a party for her? Friends who would look after her? Between her absentee and neglectful parents and a grandmother more interested in grooming a successor than raising a granddaughter, Chance could understand why Alexa didn't want to raise their child the same way. He even agreed with her, but he hated the thought of her going back to LA to live alone.

At least in Clearville Rory and Evie were around. His Aunt Evelyn had recently finished her cancer treatments and hoped to be back at work by the beginning of the New Year. Heck, even his parents were only a few hours away, too close for his comfort, but he had no doubt his mother especially was dying for a grandchild to love and—

"Whoa, there, Dad!" Nina advised, though her voice sounded far away thanks to the crazy whirlwind of thoughts circling inside his brain. "You look like you're about to pass out."

Fighting the dizzying sensation, Chance sank back against the waiting-room chair. He wasn't actually hoping Alexa might stay in Clearville… Was he?

Chance didn't know how many photographs he'd taken over the years, how many pictures he'd studied. But nothing, nothing, compared to seeing the ultrasound of his baby. He—or she—was perfect. The sex didn't matter any more than it mattered that the baby's features were little more than an indistinct blur.

This was his child.

Seeing the pictures, hearing the baby's heartbeat made it all…real in a way it hadn't been before then. He could take a thousand photos, ten thousand photos, and none of them could compare to the one he held in his hand.

"What do you think about Kylee?"

"Hmm?"

Seated together on the couch, Chance held Alexa's feet in his lap. He idly pressed his thumb into her arch. After the past few days, he'd discovered the wonder of her body again and again. He'd made a study of where to touch to make her laugh, to make her gasp, to make her moan.

But now his fingers stilled as the truth of his thoughts hit hard. Nothing would ever matter more than Alexa and their baby. And yet what was he supposed to do? Quit his job? Live off the Mayhew fortune? Everything inside him rebelled at the idea. Call him old-fashioned or chauvinistic, but he wanted to be a man who would support his family. And even if money wasn't an issue, he still craved the challenge and excitement his career offered. So not just a chauvinist, but a selfish one, as well.

"What do you think about Clearville?" he asked, still focused on the possibility that had followed him from the obstetrician's office.

Looking up from the book in her lap, an amused smile tipped her lips. Her face lit with laughter, the sound easing some of the pressure in his chest. "Well, I know parents who have named their children Paris or London, but I'm not sure I want to go with Clearville."

At his confused frown, she held up the book so he could see the title and be reminded that they were supposed to be

talking about baby names. "Sorry." He shook his head, realizing how far his mind had strayed, but he wasn't ready
to let go. Taking the book from her, he set it aside on the
coffee table. "We can talk baby names for the next four
months, but what do you think about moving to Clearville?"

"Moving? Here?" Her eyes widened at the thought, but
Chance was on a roll.

"I know Clearville doesn't have as much to offer as
LA, but it's a great small town." She'd already told him
that she didn't want their child raised by nannies and private tutors the way she had been. "A great place to raise a
family. You'd still be able to see your grandmother when
you go back for foundation events, but think about how
you've already become a part of the community here. And
between my sister and Evie and my parents, you'd have
family nearby."

Planting her palms against the cushions, Alexa sat up
straight and pulled her feet from his lap. "Your family,
Chance. Not mine."

They could be.

The thought echoed in his mind. He'd blown that first
proposal, but he'd been waiting for an opportunity to ask
Alexa a second time to marry him. But now he wouldn't
have to. She'd already given her answer.

"Oh, this looks wonderful!" Lindsay Kincaid said as
she, Rory and Alexa stepped into the parlor room decorated for her sister-in-law's baby shower.

A large circle of chairs, each tied with a cluster of blue
balloons and matching bows, surrounded a small love
seat—the place of honor for the mom-to-be. Two tables
covered in blue-and-white-striped tablecloths had been set
up against the dark walnut-paneled walls—one in anticipation of all the baby gifts, and another holding a gorgeous

cake shaped like a cradle and an assortment of finger sand-wiches, fresh cut fruits and vegetables, and a large bowl of punch. A sign overhead proclaimed It's a Boy!, and large boxes, mimicking a child's colorful toy blocks, spelled out Wyatt, the name Nina and her husband, Bryce, had picked out for their third son.

"Not that I expected anything less." Turning to Alexa, Lindsay said, "My husband, Ryder, and I were married at Hillcrest, and Rory did an amazing job!"

"It was so romantic," Rory agreed, "but I can't take credit for that. You and Ryder are the ones who made the day special. Anyone just looking could see how completely crazy you are for each other."

Lindsay's pretty face glowed with an almost secretive smile. The smile of a woman in love. A few months ago, Alexa might not have recognized it for what it was. She did now, seeing the expression every time she looked in the mirror. But unlike Lindsay, she also saw the doubt re-flected in her own eyes. She loved Chance, and while she couldn't deny he cared for her, caring wasn't love.

Pushing the troubling thought from her mind, Alexa waved a hand at the cluster of chairs. "It looks like you're expecting quite a turnout. Did you invite half the town?"

"That's the thing about living in Clearville. Everybody knows everybody." Rory rolled her eyes, but her wide smile embraced the town. "When you have an event like this, it's really hard to pick and choose who to invite…"

"So you end up inviting everybody," Lindsay chimed in. "We had thought of having the party at my in-laws'. They have a great backyard for get-togethers, but then we worried about the weather and thought we'd be better off playing it safe and partying here at Hillcrest.

"And just think," Lindsay added, "it won't be too long before we're holding one of these showers for you, Alexa."

"I, um, yes," Alexa stuttered, taken aback by the other woman's assumption that she would still be in Clearville come spring.

But as other guests began to arrive, Alexa was surprised to realize how many of the women she had already met and how many of them she was already starting to think of as friends. Along with Rory, Lindsay and Sophia, Debbie Pirelli, Sophia's sister-in-law and the owner of the Sugar & Spice café, was also in attendance. Alexa had been back for lunch at the café several times. Having met Debbie, Alexa couldn't imagine a better name for the bubbly blonde's business. Debbie was sweet, but with a sharp sense of humor that had had Alexa laughing over her chicken salad sandwich.

These women had welcomed Alexa into their circle of friendship, making her feel at home in a way she had never felt in LA even though she'd been born and raised there. Was Chance's idea of staying in Clearville really such a crazy one?

If only he hadn't made it sound like *she* would be the only one living there. But hadn't he already told her it didn't matter where he lived? After all, Chance wasn't looking for somewhere to call home. Anywhere he chose would be little more than a way station, a brief layover between flights.

And while she did appreciate how everyone had welcomed her, she couldn't help thinking he wanted to surround her with people who would *be there* so he wouldn't feel so guilty about being gone. She didn't want to add to his guilt, but she also didn't want to be a responsibility he handed off to another relative.

Been there, grown up like that.

She'd seen the disappointment in his expression when

she'd turned him down, but it wasn't Clearville that didn't have enough to offer. It was Chance.

"How are you getting Nina here without giving away the surprise?"

"That was Rory's idea," Lindsay said. "She's asked Nina to come by to give her some ideas for floral arrangements and decorations for the hotel for Christmas."

"What can I say?" Rory asked. "I'm more devious than I look."

"She'd have to be to con me into being here."

The three women turned in unison at the sound of the deep voice behind them. Alexa's heart gave a little leap at the very sight of him, and then sucked in a quick breath as she swore she felt a second flutter of movement…this time in her belly. She didn't know if it was possible, but she didn't question how her body—how her baby—responded in recognition of this man.

He was dressed in black jeans and a matching long-sleeved T-shirt, but if he thought the muted color would help him move unobtrusively among the female guests at the shower, he'd failed miserably. The soft cotton molded to broad shoulders, and the things the worn denim did for his muscular thighs and firm backside should be illegal. He looked so masculine in the purely feminine setting of the baby shower that the sheer contrast was enough to set Alexa's head spinning.

"Ha!" Rory exclaimed. "The only guy in a room full of women? Most men would consider themselves lucky."

At the word *lucky*, Chance met Alexa's gaze with a wink. "You have no idea how lucky I feel," he said before excusing himself to set up his camera.

A few minutes later, Alexa smiled as she saw another familiar face. "Summer! I almost didn't recognize you without the cowboy boots and Wranglers."

The blonde beauty held out the skirt of the geometric-print dress she wore. "A baby shower might not be an haute couture event, but I'll take what I can get."

"Is Theresa coming to the party?"

"I'm sorry to say she's not. She's been fighting the flu and didn't want to risk getting Nina or anyone else sick."

"Oh, that's too bad."

"My brother's taking good care of her. Theresa won't be able to sneeze without Jarrett there to 'God bless you.'" Summer shifted the nylon strap on her shoulder, and Alexa realized the other woman wasn't carrying a purse. Instead, a camera bag rested against her hip.

"You brought your camera."

"Oh, yeah. I take it with me everywhere. I'd feel naked without it."

Other than working at Hillcrest events, Alexa hadn't seen Chance with his camera. Was he still trying to separate his career from their life together? Or did he fear she would one day make him choose? A sick feeling settled in her stomach even as she watched from across the room as one of the women laughed at something he said.

What was it Theresa had told her?

Jarrett loved me enough to let me go.

Alexa didn't know if she had that kind of strength, but she had to find a way to love Chance McClaren—the photojournalist—as much as she loved Chance McClaren the man.

An idea of how she might start to do that sprang to mind, and she linked her arm through Summer's. "Well, I'm glad you came. After all, there's someone here you've been dying to meet."

"Looks like you just might survive."

Chance grinned at Alexa's whispered teasing, barely

audible over the constant chatter and laughter filling the parlor. "Barely. I need to talk to Rory about hazard pay."

He'd overheard more about pregnancy pains, birthing woes and breastfeeding than he ever wanted to know. And yet as Alexa's now obvious baby bump reminded him, he needed to learn. As the only man in the group, he'd also been an easy target.

"Yes, I can see a war wound. Right about here..." She reached up with a pale blue napkin, wiped at his cheek and held up the burnt-orange lipstick smudge for him to see.

Pointing at the evidence, he said, "Okay, now that was thanks to Nina's great-aunt who's a heck of a lot faster than she looks." He leaned closer to murmur, "And if we weren't trapped in this room full of women, I would be kissing you right now."

"Hitting on a pregnant lady at a baby shower, are you?"

"Only my pregnant lady."

A blush lit her cheeks at his possessive claim, and Chance stopped his teasing to take her hands in his and lace her slender fingers through his own. "Thank you, Alexa, for suggesting that Summer take over as Hillcrest's photographer. She showed me some of the work she's done on the website for her brother's ranch. She might not have much professional experience, but she definitely has talent."

Watching Summer greet almost every guest like a long-lost friend, he gave a quick laugh. "Hell, she'll probably be better at it than I was anyway."

"That is not true. Your pictures were amazing. Any couple would be lucky to have you photograph their wedding."

"Maybe but..." His words trailed off as he realized he'd spoken them before.

Alexa's mind obviously went back to that same place

and time, standing outside the cottage that first day. "This isn't your job."

"Alexa…" He searched her expression, trying to determine if he was seeing only what he wanted to see. Had Alexa somehow made peace with his career? Could she accept him for the man he was and understand the ambition and passion that drove him?

He didn't have a chance to ask as the guest of honor called for everyone's attention. "I can't thank you all enough for this." Tears filled Nina's eyes as she gazed around the room at her friends and family. "It was such a wonderful surprise, and I—I—"

"Nina?" Concern filled Lindsay's voice as her sister-in-law stopped on a sharp gasp. "Are you okay?"

"Oh!" She sucked in a breath as she braced a hand low against her belly. "Oh, my goodness… I think—I think I'm in labor."

"Okay, Dad, are you ready for this?"

Oh, thank God! Chance glanced around the waiting room, looking for a man who might be Nina's husband. He still wasn't sure how he'd ended up at the maternity ward with a woman he barely knew, but from the moment Nina made her stunning announcement in the middle of the shower, he'd been acting on instinct.

Labor equaled the delivery room at a hospital in his world, and he'd done everything he could to get Nina there as quickly as possible. He ignored her suggestion that Lindsay drive her home first to grab the overnight bag she had packed and waiting for her scheduled delivery. He overrode Lindsay's suggestion that they try to get ahold of Bryce to pick Nina up at the hotel. He shook off Rory's quiet suggestion that they call 9-1-1 and wait for an ambulance.

His plan was clear. Labor=hospital. Do not pass go. Do not collect two hundred dollars.

Lindsay and Nina's younger sister had ridden along, Jessie sitting in the back of the SUV with Nina while Lindsay rode shotgun. At first he'd been glad to have the two other women along to keep Nina calm… Until Lindsay kept warning him to slow down and not drive like a bat out of hell when he was only doing fifty miles an hour, and Jessie and Nina were bickering over whether emailed thank-you notes for the baby gifts were appropriate or far too impersonal.

He spent the forty-five-minute drive to the hospital in Redfield with his hands clenched on the wheel, fighting the urge to remind the three of them that a baby was on its way!

And then Nina had wanted to walk into the hospital when she clearly needed a wheelchair to get her inside as soon as possible. When she slowed to breathe through a contraction, Chance had put an end to her waddling pace and scooped her into his arms.

He wanted to hand off responsibility the moment the doors swept open, but even after telling the nurse at the admittance desk *repeatedly* that a woman was in labor, said nurse repeatedly told *him* to have the patient fill out a stack of forms at least an inch thick.

Chance had been in enough hospitals over the years to know they were nothing like depicted on television, but he would have given just about anything for a white-coated physician to sweep Nina up onto a gurney and rush her down a hallway yelling "Stat!" and "Code Blue!" at the top of their lungs.

But the only doctor in sight was the one looking directly at him…

Oh, crap.

Chance glanced down at Nina, but she was breathing through another contraction and gripping his hand like a vise. And while he was glad to see she was finally taking this whole thing seriously, he needed her to throw him a lifeline here. "No! I'm not the dad. At least not her dad. I mean, her baby's dad."

Lindsay had been trying to get ahold of Bryce, but Nina's husband had been in on the surprise baby shower and had taken their two boys off on a father-son adventure to free their mom up for the afternoon. Chance's panicked gaze shot across the waiting room to where Lindsay was pacing back and forth. Judging by the cell still raised to her ear, she hadn't yet reached Nina's husband.

"That's okay. We have all kinds of relatives and friends of the family acting as a birthing coach."

Birthing coach? If not for the killer grip Nina had on his hand, Chance had the feeling he would have bolted from the waiting room, in his haste bowling over the slightly wild-eyed man coming through the automatic doors. Only what kind of man would he be if he left a pregnant woman in need? What kind of father would he be if he left the woman pregnant with his child?

"Nina, babe!"

The dark-haired man who'd rushed into the waiting room dropped to his knees in front of Nina's chair. "Hey, sweetheart. You doing okay?"

Opening her eyes, Nina smiled at her husband as if he'd been at her side the whole time. "Oh, Bryce! Lindsay threw me the most amazing baby shower. You should see all of the cute presents…" A troubled frown tightened her forehead. "Lindsay, what did you do with the presents?"

"They're still at the hotel, sweetie." Her mission accomplished, Lindsay had stuck her phone back in her purse.

"Well, we can't just leave them there. Bryce, you should go—"

"No!" Chance and Bryce shouted out in unison.

Carefully extracting his hand from Nina's, Chance transferred her bone-crushing grip to her husband. "I'll go back to the hotel and make sure the gifts are all taken care of. You stay here and...focus on having that baby."

Catching Lindsay's eye, he asked, "You'll be okay here?"

She nodded. "We have a ton of family on the way. We'll be fine. Thank you, Chance. I think this goes pretty far beyond the realm of baby shower photographer."

"Now Rory really owes me that hazard pay."

The pretty blonde laughed and patted his shoulder "You should be thanking her."

"Thanking her?" He was hoping he didn't throttle his sister the next time he saw her.

Tipping her head toward Bryce and Nina huddled together in a world of their own, she said, "You can consider it practice. For when you *are* the baby's dad."

After the exciting finish to the baby shower, Alexa stayed and helped Rory move all of the presents into a small storage room and clean up the parlor for the next event. "You do know how to throw one heck of a baby shower," Alexa told Rory once they sank into a pair of chairs to finish off the last of the cake.

"Here at Hillcrest, we aim to please."

Lindsay had called earlier to reassure them that Chance had gotten Nina to the hospital and that Bryce had shown up not long after. It would still be a while before the baby made his appearance into the world, but the doctors were confident everything would go well.

"Note to self," Alexa said as she dug into the strawberry and cream cake. "Have baby shower well before the due date."

"Hmm, good idea. Any chance that there will be a bridal shower before that baby shower?"

Nearly choking on the bite of cake, Alexa reached for her cup of punch. Buying some time, she sipped at the sweet, berry-flavored drink. "Did Chance tell you he asked me to marry him?"

Rory nodded. "And that you turned him down."

"I know Chance wants to be a good father to our baby, but we won't have to get married for that to happen."

"Did you ever wonder if maybe what he really wants is to be a good husband?" Rory reached over and squeezed her hand. "And he does have to get married for that."

Alexa took another drink, but all the punch in the world wouldn't ease the sudden ache in her throat. She knew Chance cared about her, but could she believe that he loved her? Enough to want to marry her even if she wasn't carrying his baby?

What had Chance said about his reasons for not wanting to show his work at Roslynn St. Clare's gallery, about not trusting that the woman was interested in him for his own sake?

I'll never know for sure, will I?

Chapter Fifteen

A drizzling rain accompanied Chance and Alexa to Rory and Jamison's house on Thanksgiving Day. The couple was renting a house outside of town until their own custom home was completed, but Rory had insisted on having the meal at their place. With the windshield wipers a steady, quiet *swoosh* against the glass and the heater blowing at her feet, Alexa should have felt happy, content.

The baby fluttered in her belly, and Chance reached over to smooth his hand over her royal blue cashmere sweater. She didn't know how he seemed to know whenever the baby moved, but he did. A trained observer, Chance made his living watching people, and she probably had some slight tell that gave it away, but it seemed like more than that. Like the baby bonds tying them together were so strong that he just *knew*.

Despite that connection, Alexa couldn't help feeling like he was pulling away from her. He'd been quiet ever since the baby shower a few days earlier. Lindsay had called to let everyone know that mother and son were doing fine. She'd told Alexa that Chance had been rock solid on the way to the hospital, then sitting at Nina's side until Bryce arrived and staying until the baby was born.

But Chance had hardly said more than a few words since.

Rory welcomed them inside with a hug, accepting the fall floral arrangement of peach roses, burgundy carnations and butterscotch daisies that Chance carried before showing them where to hang their damp coats. The house was cozy and warm, with the sound of a football game playing in the background and the scents of roasting turkey along with a mix of sage and cinnamon and cloves filling the air.

Chance introduced Alexa to Hannah, the adorable daughter of Rory's fiancé, to Evie's parents and to Evie's namesake, Evelyn.

"She's recently gone through chemo," Chance told Alexa quietly in explanation of the colorful scarf wrapped around the slender woman's head. "Her tests have come back negative, and she's cancer-free."

"Definitely something to be thankful for," she whispered back.

"So where's that other niece of mine?" Evelyn asked Rory, who rolled her eyes.

"'Hillcrest House does not take holidays,'" she said in perfect imitation of her somewhat uptight cousin. In a normal tone, she added, "You know Evie, Aunt E. She's so like you."

Evelyn fingered the end of her scarf. "Yes, that's exactly what I'm afraid of."

"If it isn't the man of the hour," Rory's fiancé, Jamison, announced as he walked into the room, a bottle lifted in a toast. "Everyone's talking about Nina's baby shower and your wild rush to the hospital."

Though he accepted a beer from the other man, Chance shook his head. "I didn't do much, believe me, and thank God for it!"

Wrapping her arms around Jamison's waist, Rory smiled. "Well, clearly Nina and Bryce don't share your opinion. Otherwise why would they have named their baby Wyatt Chance Kincaid?"

"They named him after you?" Alexa looked up at Chance in surprise, but he only shrugged in response, having clearly already heard the news. "Why didn't you tell me?"

His attention focused on the beer in his hand, he shrugged again. "Like I said, it was no big deal. I was just…"

There.

His voice trailed off, the unspoken word a very big deal between the two of them.

He made it through dinner. He sat with his family as his father said grace. He dished up food, passed along plates and compliments as they all dived into the traditional Thanksgiving feast.

But as Rory and Jamison were clearing the dinner plates for dessert, he'd made his escape. Chance couldn't really call it anything else. Stepping out onto the front porch, he sucked in a much-needed lungful of cool, rain-scented air.

The man of the hour.

Chance knew Jamison meant the words as a teasing compliment, but he couldn't help feeling like the other man had hit the time frame right on the dot. An hour, he could do. A lifetime commitment? The kind Bryce had made to Nina? The kind Jamison had made to Rory and to his daughter by walking away from a lucrative job as a corporate attorney for life in small town Clearville?

That was something Chance didn't know if he was capable of.

He swallowed hard. How had Alexa described her parents?

They were like Christmas and New Year's and the Fourth of July...

He'd been there for Thanksgiving. If he took the assignment his editor had offered, he'd be lucky to be back with Alexa by Christmas.

The screen door squeaked behind him, and Chance turned to see his father in the doorway. Matthew paused, his split-second hesitation—a hesitation Chance had caused by walking away too many times—hitting hard.

A sudden image of Alexa making pancakes flashed in his mind. She was willing to try, to work hard, not to follow in her parents' selfish, self-absorbed footsteps. Chance wanted to be a good father. Maybe his first step was in trying to be a better son.

"Hey, Dad. Wanna join me?"

Taking Chance up on the offer, Matthew stepped outside. For a moment, the two men stood silently side by side, the drip of rainwater from the eaves the only sound.

"You might want to get back in there before everyone's done fighting over that last piece of pie," Matthew said after a moment.

"I'll head back in after a minute. What about you? You've never been one to turn down dessert."

His father made a sound that might have been a laugh. "And your mother knows it. She cut me a slice so thin, it was practically see-through." He sighed. "I just needed a minute or two for myself."

They'd always had that in common, Chance realized.

A need for space. How many times as a kid had he found his father sitting by himself on their back patio? Matthew had found room to breathe in his own backyard. Chance's need had taken him a hell of a lot farther.

"You're walking better than the last time we were here," his father pointed out.

"Yes."

"I take it that means you'll be heading out on another assignment soon."

Chance opened his mouth to give another affirmative, but the words didn't come. Instead he found himself saying, "I want to explain why I've been—distant these last few months," he began before relaying the conversation he'd overheard in the hospital when they'd thought he was still asleep.

"Chance. What you heard…" His father scrubbed a hand along his jaw before clasping the back of his neck. "It wasn't what you thought you heard."

"I may have been whacked out on pain killers, but I know what I heard." Sucking in a deep breath, he added, "But I also want you to know that I…understand a little better now. When I think of anything happening to Alexa or the baby, well, I guess I can see where you were coming from in wanting to keep me safe."

"Your mother and I weren't just worried about you being safe, Chance. We were worried about you being *happy*," his father stressed.

"You thought I wasn't happy? Dad, I have the career I've always dreamed of, a job I love—"

"Do you?" his father challenged. "Do you still love it? Because over the past few years, your mother and I have both started to wonder. Not that your work has ever suffered. Your photos and the articles you've written are as inspired and as passionate as ever, but we've gotten the feeling that the demands of the job, the constant traveling, have started to take a toll."

Chance wanted to argue just—he feared—for the sake of the argument. Hadn't he started to question his commitment ever since meeting Alexa? Had his parents sensed he was burning out even earlier than that? How many times he had pushed through sheer exhaustion, times when he woke up not sure what country he was in, forget what city, by forcing himself to put one foot in front of the other?

Grabbing the railing with both hands, Chance stared out over the rain-soaked yard. "I can't go back to Medford, Dad. I know how much you love the shop but—"

Matthew interrupted with a snort of laughter. "Get a grip, son. I gave up that dream a long time ago."

"So you aren't still hoping that I'll take over?"

"Is that what I wished for when you first took an interest in photography? Sure. And I know I made the mistake of pushing too hard and ended up pushing you away. You ran off to prove that you could make it as a photographer, and you've done that. We just want you to slow down long enough to ask yourself if the life you're living is still the one you want. Or if maybe there's something more."

A rare smile softened his father's features, and Chance followed his old man's gaze to see a tiny red tricycle parked in the corner of the porch. "Your life has changed, son. You have…so much more to live for."

Chance scowled. "That makes it sound as if I didn't want to live before. Like you think I had some kind of death wish."

"Of course not. But you were reckless. You took chances other journalists wouldn't take because you only had yourself to worry about." He held up a hand before Chance could protest again. "I'm not saying you didn't care about us, but a wife and child are different. Alexa and the baby need you more."

The weight on his chest pressed harder as he admitted, "I don't know if I can just walk away. This life—being a photojournalist, it's the only job I've ever known, the only job I've ever wanted."

Matthew gave another short laugh. "You need to take a look at this." Reaching into his back pocket, he pulled out a piece of paper and unfolded it to reveal a crayon-colored picture of a lopsided, slightly turquoise Christmas tree. "As soon as Hannah saw your mother and me this morning, she wanted us to have this. It's her Christmas list, one I'm pretty sure Rory helped with since Hannah isn't old enough to write yet. But she's old enough to let her soon-to-be grandparents know that she wants a doll, a paint set and some computer game I've never heard of."

"That's great, Dad, but I'm not really sure what that has to do with anything."

After tucking the list back into his pocket, his father asked, "Do you remember what you asked for when you were five?"

"What?" His mother had always been the sentimental type, holding on to pieces of the past he'd long since forgotten, not his father. "No, Dad…"

"When you were five," he said, undeterred by his interruption, "you wanted one of those glow sword things… What were they called?"

"Lightsabers. I wanted a lightsaber."

"Right. And then when you were seven, you wanted a baseball bat and glove, and a Mariners hat."

Chance gave a short laugh, getting caught up in reminiscing despite himself. "We'd gone to a few games that past season, and I thought I was going to be the next Ken Griffey Jr."

"So you didn't always want to be a photojournalist."

"Maybe not, but, Dad, I was never going to be a Jedi warrior—lightsaber or no lightsaber."

"That is not the point." Reaching out, Matthew clapped him on the shoulder. "The point is that dreams change over the years. By the time you were a teenager, you knew you wanted to be a photographer. You followed that dream, you worked hard for that dream and you succeeded. But that was then. This is now. And walking away from that— if it's what you choose to do—that isn't quitting. You aren't giving up on your dreams, Chance. You're just... dreaming bigger."

The bedroom was still dark when Alexa woke, but she knew even before she reached across the mattress what had disturbed her. Chance was no longer lying beside her. Slipping out from beneath the blankets, she walked down the hall. She must have made some slight sound at the sight of him standing in the living room. He spun to face her—a familiar olive drab duffel bag in his hand.

"You're leaving?"

"My editor called—" Chance swore as he dropped the bag and crossed the room to catch her by the shoulders. "You're as white as a sheet."

"I'm fine. I'm just..." Her voice trailed off as he led her to the sofa. Sinking into the cushions, she closed her eyes. The image was seared on her eyelids—Chance holding that same duffel in their Santa Barbara hotel room before telling her he had to go.

"I have to do this, Lexi." Kneeling in front of her, he covered her clenched fists with his hands. "You knew I would take another assignment at some point."

She had known. But seeing him with that duffel bag... It had been her last memory of him, the one she'd carried with her for all those weeks until she read the news reports that said he'd been killed. She swallowed hard, forcing the ache in her throat to sink into a painful knot in her stomach.

"I thought we would at least discuss it first! What the assignment is, how long you'll be gone, where you'll be going..."

How dangerous it would be...

"I swear, Alexa, I won't be gone long, and when I'm back, I'll—"

"Call?" she filled in. After all, they had played this scene once before. She knew how it ended. With Chance grabbing his things and leaving her behind—hurt, angry and determined to harden her heart.

She didn't even know why she thought this time might be different, but that same toxic mix of emotions was already building inside her chest. Is that how it would always be? Chance resenting her for asking him to stay while she resented him for telling her he had to go?

"Were you even going to tell me you were leaving or were you planning to sneak out and avoid any messy farewells?"

"That's not fair, Alexa."

"Not fair?" Pulling her hand from his, she pointed at the duffel bag and demanded, "You want to talk about not fair? Your editor just called, but tell me, Chance, how long has that bag been packed and ready to go? Days? Weeks?"

His jaw tightened in response, revealing the answer he wouldn't give, and that knot inside her tripled.

Her voice thick with unshed tears, she whispered, "I can live with you being gone, Chance, but what I can't take is for you to have one foot out the door even when you're here."

Chance flinched as if she'd struck him. "That's not—do

you want to know why I had that bag packed, why I didn't stop to talk to you about the assignment before I said yes? I knew if I slowed down for even a second, that if I didn't leave now, I never would!"

He ducked his head, his voice barely audible as he confessed, "I'm afraid, Alexa."

Her heart ached at the pained admission. "Of course you are, Chance! Who wouldn't be after what happened last time?"

"I'm not afraid for me," he said as he shook his head. "What if something happens to you while I'm gone? What if something happens to the baby?"

He looked up then, and Alexa forgot how to breathe. Forgot…everything for a second, held spellbound by the vulnerability she never would have thought she'd see. Linking his fingers with hers, he held on tight as if he'd never let her go.

Faint wings of hope fluttered within her chest as she whispered, "Oh, Chance… I can't promise you that nothing will happen to me." Even as tears filled her eyes, she gave a small laugh at the reversal of roles. Wasn't she the one who was supposed to be afraid of losing him? Wasn't he the one who was supposed to reassure her?

And yet wasn't that what loving someone could do? Make you vulnerable and yet invincible? Weak and yet strong. Overjoyed and terrified, all at the same time.

"But you've shown me that some risks are worth taking and some of the best things in life are unplanned. Like meeting you, like this baby…like falling in love."

His throat moved as he swallowed, and he opened his mouth but the words didn't come. Disappointment tugged at her heart, but Alexa refused to allow the emotion to take hold. Maybe, maybe admitting how he felt would leave Chance too vulnerable. Maybe it was her turn to be strong. Strong enough to let him go and strong enough to believe he would return.

He took a step back as she stood. "Alexa—"

Reaching up, she cupped his face in her hands. "It's all right. I'll be right back."

It didn't take her long to find what she was looking for in the tiny bedroom. Chance was standing where she had left him, and Alexa didn't know if she'd ever seen him so still. As if on the edge of a crumbling precipice, not knowing which way to turn.

So different from the man she'd met in Santa Barbara, the one who'd known exactly where he was going, the one whose steps were confident and sure—even as he'd walked away from her.

That was the man she needed him to be. The man who could shut off his emotions with the single-minded purpose of getting his shot. The man who could keep his head in the game and who would survive and come back to her.

"Here." Slipping her hand into his, she pressed the butterfly hairpin into his palm. "It's your good-luck charm, remember? I want you to take it with you, and then I want—I want you to bring it back to me."

Chapter Sixteen

"So, Alexa." Seated at a table in the Hillcrest dining room, Virginia Mayhew pinned Alexa with her piercing blue gaze. "Where is this young man of yours?"

Focusing on the grilled salmon she had no desire to eat, Alexa said, "He had to leave on a business trip. I'm sorry, Grandmother. I know how you hate to travel."

Virginia sniffed as she smoothed a napkin over her silk skirt. "Well, thank goodness for private planes. Had I been forced to fly commercial, I'd be tempted to chase after him and give him a piece of my mind."

A small smile tugged at the corners of her mouth at the idea of her grandmother dressing Chance down in some middle of nowhere dot on the map.

Seeing the McClaren family together at Thanksgiving, Alexa had known she needed to call her grandmother to tell her about the baby. This was not just her child. This was Virginia's great-grandchild.

Alexa had been dreading telling her grandmother she was pregnant, fearing how her somewhat old-fashioned, austere grandmother might react. But Virginia had surprised her. After a moment of stunned silence, she had offered her genuine congratulations. And then she'd caught Alexa completely off guard with her offer to travel to Clearville to meet Chance.

Something she'd wanted to surprise him with and then completely forgot about when he told her he was leaving. But he would be back. He'd meet her grandmother some other time. Alexa held on to that belief with her whole heart.

"I'm so sorry you came all this way for nothing—"

"I came all this way for *you*, Alexa. Yes, I wanted to meet the father of your child, but I came to see you. I've missed you."

"I don't think you've ever said that before."

"You never left before." Even though a hint of reproach entered Virginia's voice, she shook her head. "And that's my fault."

"I don't understand."

"You're a grown woman, Alexa. You should have married and started your own family years ago. Instead you've spent the last two decades living— Well, not just living with an old woman, but living *like* an old woman."

"That's not—entirely true," Alexa protested, her weekend with Chance—and all that followed—the exception that proved the rule.

"You're in love with him, aren't you?" her grandmother asked.

"I do love him, but—"

"You're afraid."

"I— Yes, how did you know?"

Virginia sighed. "Because I've spent most of my life

feeling that same way. The exact same way I've taught you to live. Always afraid to trust. Always afraid to love." Her blue eyes filled with regret as she confessed, "And I am sorry for that, Alexa."

"Grandmother, no. You've taught me so much! About business, about the foundation."

Her grandmother waved a blue-veined hand. "Business, yes. I've taught you about business. But about life? About love? I'm afraid that is where I've failed miserably." Virginia signaled a server to box up the food neither of them had much interest in eating.

After the young woman swept the table clear and brought hot water for their tea, she said, "I know you don't remember your grandfather. He died while you were still a baby, but he was the love of my life. And your father was his spitting image. In ways that were both fortunate and unfortunate."

"I'm sorry I don't remember him." Alexa warmed her hands on the ceramic mug, fascinated by this side of her grandmother she had never seen before.

"They both had such energy. Lighting a room simply by stepping foot inside. I never felt as truly alive as I did when I was with your grandfather. And when he died—and then your father and mother died only a few years later… Somehow they took all that light, all that life with them."

Virginia shook her head and reached for a packet of sugar, her movement brisk and efficient as she poured the sweetener into her tea. Her voice crisp and matter-of-fact even as she admitted, "I was devastated. I didn't know how I'd go on without them, and to my shame, for a long time, I didn't want to."

As a child, Alexa had thought only of her own loss. Her mother, her father…gone. She hadn't stopped to think of Virginia's loss. It had seemed to her, at the time, as though her grandmother hadn't cared. Now, as an adult, she could better understand that Virginia had cared too much. "I'm so sorry, Grandmother."

"I wish I had been strong enough to show you how to move on, but instead I was stuck in my own sorrow. I hope someday you can forgive me for that."

"There's nothing to forgive. I loved them, too, but my parents were—unpredictable to say the least. I needed someone I could count on. Needed you."

"I hope that's true, Alexa. But it's time for you to live your own life now. Don't let your fear of losing love keep you from grabbing it with both hands and holding on tight."

Some risks are worth taking…like falling in love.

Alexa's voice echoed through his thoughts as Chance paced the waiting area at the San Francisco airport. Louder than his fellow passengers wheeling by with luggage, louder than the conversations carried on by people with cell phones all around him, louder than the distant roar of the airplane engines.

He'd made the long drive from Clearville at a record pace, not stopping to give himself time to think, only to arrive at check-in and discover the city's frequent fog had delayed the inbound plane.

Leaving him with nothing to do but wait…and think.

She loved him. Alexa had all but said the words, and in return he'd left her. Walked away from the woman carrying his child. The woman who loved him.

The woman *he* loved.

All his life he'd lived on the edge. He relished adventure and excitement. Willing to take the greatest risk for the greatest reward.

God, he was such a fraud!

Chance bent over in the chair, elbows braced on his

knees. He was brave enough to put his life on the line, but when it came to his heart? When it came to telling Alexa how he felt, he'd been a total coward.

He glanced at his watch. Damn, had his battery died? It couldn't be—but a quick look at the digital clock behind the flight attendant's station confirmed that only five minutes had passed.

After trying to sit for a few minutes with his knee jittering like a jackhammer, Chance shot to his feet. Paced. Sat. Paced some more.

"Settle down, son," the elderly man seated a few chairs away said. "No need for all this commotion. Flying's the safest way to travel."

He wasn't afraid to fly. He'd never been afraid to fly. So why was he suddenly so…terrified?

The intercom crackled, but instead of hearing the announcement, his father's voice echoed through his mind. *We just want you to slow down long enough to ask yourself if the life you're living is still the one you want.*

Slow down… The jackhammering in his leg came to a gradual stop as Chance sucked in a deep breath and asked himself if there was something he wanted more.

"I don't want to leave."

He didn't realize he'd spoken the words out loud until the old man glanced over his wire-framed reading glasses and said, "Well, then, maybe an airport isn't the best place for you to be."

The vibration of his cell phone shot Chance from the chair once more, and he scrambled to pull it from his pocket. His crazily racing heart sank when an unfamiliar number flashed across the screen. "Hello?"

"Mr. McClaren, my name is Roslynn St. Clare. You don't know me, but I own an art gallery in Beverly Hills and I saw some of your work at the Mayhew charity auction a few months ago."

"Ms. St. Clare, this is a surprise."

"A good one, I hope, once you hear what I have to say. It turns out I have an opening in the New Year and would like to showcase your work. We can finalize the details with your agent later, but I wanted to speak with you personally first. It will be a solo show, of course, as befitting your talent with a four-week run."

Listening as the woman discussed the impressive terms, Chance knew most photographers would jump at the opportunity. But he couldn't accept an offer he wasn't 100 percent certain he'd earned.

"I'm sorry, Ms. St. Clare. I don't know what Alexa told you, but I'm not interested in a gallery show."

Judging by the silence that followed, Chance figured not many people turned down a woman like Roslynn St. Clare. "I don't know what it is you *think* Alexa Mayhew told me. We discussed your work the night of the auction, but I had another engagement and had to leave before you arrived. I am sorry we didn't get to meet that night and—"

"Wait," Chance interrupted, "you spoke to Alexa that night? At the auction?"

Before he and Alexa had even met? Before she would have had any possible reason to suggest a showing of his photographs other than a real and *honest* appreciation of his work?

After another silence, the gallery owner stated, "You seem somewhat distracted, Mr. McClaren. Why don't you get with your agent and take a day or so to think about my offer and get back to me?"

But as Roslynn ended the call, Chance wasn't thinking about getting back to her. All he could think about was getting back to Alexa.

* * *

"What do you mean Alexa's gone?" Chance stalked after his cousin as she walked through the lobby, ever-present tablet in hand.

"I mean, she…left." Evie stopped to examine the display of brochures touting local businesses and upcoming Clearville events before making a note with her stylus on the glowing screen. It took every ounce of self-control he possessed not to jerk the damn thing from her hands and chuck it clear into the Pacific.

"She left."

Giving an exasperated sigh, she turned to face him. "Alexa is gone. Alexa has left. And repeating everything I say doesn't change that."

"Fine. *When* did she leave? I was only gone—"

"Oh, that's right. *You* were gone. And nope, repeating that doesn't change things either, does it?"

He should have known Evie wouldn't cut him any slack, not after her own less than stellar romantic history. After practically being left at the altar, she didn't think too highly of men who bailed.

"Her grandmother arrived and they left together."

"Her—" Chance stopped himself before he could echo Evie yet again.

"Yes, Virginia Mayhew flew in on a private jet, had a limo, and a bodyguard roughly the size of the Hulk, the whole 'crazy rich' nine yards."

"Her grandmother came to take her home?"

"No, actually, she came to meet you, the father of Alexa's baby, only…" Her voice trailed off with a pointed look as she waited for him.

"I was gone," he filled in on cue.

Years ago, he'd been in a plane that had lost altitude, plunging thousands of feet in seconds. That was nothing compared to the way his stomach dropped now. Alexa had all but said she loved him and what had he done? Walked out on her in return. And then he'd expected, what? For her to just sit around and wait for him to come back?

He swore beneath his breath. "I screwed up, Evie."

"That you did." Softening her stance slightly, she held out her tablet and said, "But you can't fix it while she's there and you're here."

Looking at the screen, Chance saw an airline website and a list of flights to LA.

"Oh, my gosh! Isn't this just…spectacular?"

Alexa managed a smile as Raquel rose on tiptoe and craned her neck to take in the glitz and glamour of the hotel ballroom. Gowns of every color gleamed beneath the golden chandelier, the light reflecting on the flash of rubies, emeralds and diamonds. Laughter and the clink of champagne flutes filled the air as the guests mingled together.

"And you look amazing! Have I told you how totally unfair it is that you look sexier pregnant than I do after dieting for the past three months?"

Alexa smoothed a hand along the skirt of her off-the-shoulder seafoam green gown. Having just hit the eighteen-week mark, the chiffon folds of the empire waist didn't quite hide her baby bump. "You don't need to diet. Most women would kill for your curves."

"I still can't believe I'm here with all these famous people!" Her grandmother's assistant looked stunning in a violet halter-style gown that complemented her dark hair and olive skin. Seeming to catch herself, Raquel sank back down on her heels and added, "And, um, it's for such a worthy cause."

"You've done a wonderful job." While Alexa had done

the initial work organizing the Giving Thanks benefit, Raquel had proved herself over the past few weeks. Alexa had no doubt that she was leaving her grandmother in good hands.

"We both know I couldn't have pulled this off without you laying the groundwork. And I can't tell you how much I appreciate all the faith you've put in me."

Alexa's heart tugged a little at the younger woman's words, but the sentimental moment ended as Raquel grabbed her arm with a gasp. "Did you see who just walked in?" A meteor shower of camera flashes announced the arrival of the latest Hollywood heartthrob. "Do you think I could go meet him? Just to, you know…"

"Welcome him on behalf of the Mayhew Foundation?" Alexa suggested wryly.

"Yes! Yes, that is exactly what I will do. I will *welcome* him." Straightening her shoulders, Raquel smoothed her hands over her skirt before giving one last half-swallowed squeal of excitement. "He is *so* hot!"

Chuckling to herself, Alexa watched Raquel cross the ballroom to meet the famous actor. Despite whatever fan-girl nerves she might have felt inside, the young woman was the epitome of professionalism as she shook the man's hand and thanked him for his support.

"She's right, you know."

Alexa glanced over her shoulder as her grandmother joined her. "I had no idea you were such an action-star fan."

"Don't be impertinent, young lady," Virginia scolded, but a small smile tugged at her grandmother's lined lips. "We couldn't have done this without you. It's a fitting farewell."

Tears scratched at the back of her throat. "It's not like I'm leaving the foundation."

On the trip back to LA, Alexa had talked to her grandmother about doing more, being more than simply the face of the foundation. How she wanted to be more hands-on, game-planning for how the money raised could be put to use and seeing at ground level the results of what all that hard work had brought to fruition.

The words had rushed out of her on a single breath of air, leaving her a little light-headed. Discussing her ideas with Lindsay and Theresa in Clearville was one thing. Bringing them up to her grandmother had been something else entirely.

But her grandmother had surprised her once more. "You're a Mayhew, Alexa. There is nothing a Mayhew can't do."

Alexa had laughed at that. After all the years of what a Mayhew didn't do…

Gazing around the ballroom, Virginia said, "I'm looking forward to seeing your efforts come to life, Alexa. But for now, I think there's a certain action movie star I would like to meet. From what I've heard, he's…hot."

Her smile faded as her grandmother walked away, leaving Alexa by herself in the ballroom. It was impossible to ignore the memories of the last time she was on her own in a gilded ballroom, surrounded by wealthy and famous people.

"Can I have this dance?"

Alexa froze, certain she was imaging things. Because the deep voice sending chills down her spine sounded just like… Slowly turning around, her breath caught in her throat. "Chance!"

He looked heart-stoppingly gorgeous in a black tuxedo, the onyx buttons marching down his chest a sharp contrast to the crisp white shirt. "This is our song, isn't it?" He stood with his hands casually tucked in his pockets, but a hint of nerves gave him away. His right hand twitched, rippling the material of his trousers.

"What—what are you doing here? What happened with your assignment?"

"I'm here because this is where you are and because I wanted to give you this." He withdrew his hand from his pocket, but instead of holding out the butterfly hairpin, he held a ring. A princess-cut diamond in a platinum art deco setting sparkled beneath the crystal chandelier, stunning in its simplicity.

"Chance…"

"If you don't like it, you can always pick out something else."

She couldn't imagine finding a ring she would like more. "It's beautiful, but I—" Her voice broke on the word, but she held her head high. She and her grandmother might have come to an understanding, but not everything had changed. There were still some things a Mayhew did not do. Including having a meltdown in the middle of a charity event. "I know how important your job is to you. How much it is a part of you—"

"You're right. It is a part of me, but only a small part. When it comes to you and our baby, I'm all in. Not just both feet, but heart and soul," he vowed. "I talked to Roslynn St. Clare. Thankfully the woman is used to dealing with temperamental artists, so even if she does think I'm a complete whack job, she's still willing to work with me on a showing."

Her heart pounded as she tried to grasp hold of what his acceptance might mean, and Chance wasn't done yet.

"I've looked at the dark side of life through my camera lens for too long. I want to focus on the good. Like the work done by the charities the Mayhew Foundation supports. The schools and clinics and shelters."

The elegant ballroom seemed to twirl in a crazy kaleidoscope as Alexa's head spun dizzily. Chance's vision of his future so perfectly matched her own that she couldn't have planned it better if she tried. "Are you sure, Chance? That you'll be happy…"

"With you? With our baby? Nothing could make me happier." He flashed her a smile that was one part cocky, one part nerves as he said, "Except maybe you saying you'll marry me."

"Oh, Chance."

"I love you, Alexa. I should have said it before…"

"You're saying it now, that's all that matters." The emotion in his eyes sparkled as brightly as the lights reflecting in the diamond ring, but one lingering doubt held her back. "What—what would you do if I wasn't pregnant?"

"If you weren't pregnant?" His expression gentled as he gazed down at her. "Is that what you're worried about? You shouldn't be because that's an easy question to answer. If you weren't pregnant, I'd do my damnedest to get you that way."

Pure pleasure rippled through her at the sensual promise. "Well, it's not like you can get me more pregnant."

His teeth flashed in a dimpled grin. "That's no reason not to keep trying. But the next time you're in my bed, I would very much like to be making love to my wife."

"I love you, Chance, and yes, I will marry you!"

After slipping the ring on her finger, Chance pulled her into his arms, and Alexa forgot all about what a Mayhew did not do as he kissed her in a ballroom filled with people. He held her tight as if they'd been apart for months, and she knew that no matter how far he might travel, he would always be with her. In the love she held in her heart. In the child they created together.

When Chance swept her into his arms beneath a sparkling chandelier all those months ago, Alexa would never have imagined he would be the man she would love, the man she would marry...

Life would never be without risks, but this was one chance she would never regret taking.

* * * * *

Will permanent-skeptic Evie McClaren finally meet her perfect match?

Don't miss the next installment in Stacy Connelly's miniseries Hillcrest House *Coming fall 2019, Wherever Harlequin books and ebooks are sold.*

And look for Rory's story, The Best Man Takes a Bride *Available now!*

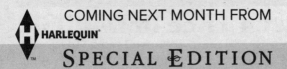

COMING NEXT MONTH FROM

HARLEQUIN®

SPECIAL EDITION

Available September 18, 2018

#2647 UNMASKING THE MAVERICK
Montana Mavericks: The Lonelyhearts Ranch • by Teresa Southwick
Rugged former marine Brendan Tanner recently moved to Rust Creek Falls and is shocked by the sparks that fly between him and Fiona O'Reilly. They're both gun-shy when it comes to love, but maybe Fiona will succeed in unmasking this maverick's heart!

#2648 ALMOST A BRAVO
The Bravos of Valentine Bay • by Christine Rimmer
Aislinn Bravo just found out she was switched at birth—and to fulfill her biological father's will, she must marry Jaxon Winters. She thought she had buried any feelings for Jaxon long ago, but when they're forced to spend three months as husband and wife, those feelings come roaring back to the surface.

#2649 SECOND CHANCE IN STONE CREEK
Maggie & Griffin • by Michelle Major
No matter how much mayor Maggie Spencer avoids bad boy Griffin Stone, there's only so far to go in Stonecreek. Only so long she can deny an undeniable attraction. Their families are feuding, the gossip is threatening her reelection, but nothing can keep her away...

#2650 THE RANCHER'S CHRISTMAS PROMISE
Return to the Double C • by Allison Leigh
Ryder Wilson is determined to make a home for the baby his late estranged wife left on a stranger's doorstep. Local lawyer Greer Templeton is there to help. It's enough to make Ryder propose a marriage of convenience. But does love factor into his Christmas promise?

#2651 THE TEXAS COWBOY'S QUADRUPLETS
Texas Legends: The McCabes • by Cathy Gillen Thacker
Mitzi Martin is desperate to save her newly inherited business—while raising infant quadruplets! Chase McCabe only wants to help but their previous broken engagement makes it difficult to convince Mitzi he's sincere. Can he save her business and convince Mitzi to give him another chance?

#2652 THE CAPTAINS' VEGAS VOWS
American Heroes • by Caro Carson
An impromptu Vegas wedding lands two army captains in married quarters while they wait for the ninety-day waiting period required to get a divorce. She thinks she's not cut out for marriage and he doesn't believe in love. Will ninety days be enough to find their happily-ever-after?

HSECNM0918

"So, the boot is finally on the other foot."

Mitzy Martin stared at the indomitable CEO standing on
the other side of her front door, looking more rancher than
businessman in nice-fitting jeans, boots and a tan Western
shirt. Ignoring the skittering of her heart, she heaved a sigh
to convey just how unwelcome he was. "What's your point,
cowboy?"

Mischief gleaming in his smoky-blue eyes, Chase looked
her up and down in a way that made her insides flutter. "Just
that you've been a social worker in Laramie County for
what…ten years now?"

Electricity sparked between them with all the danger of
a downed power line. "Eleven," Mitzy corrected. And it had
been slightly longer than that. Since she'd abruptly ended
their engagement…

"My guess is, very few people are happy to see you
coming up their front walk. Now you seem to be feeling
that," he continued with an ornery grin, "seeing *me* at your
door."

Mitzy drew a breath, ignoring the considerable physical
awareness that never failed to materialize between them.

She gave him a long, level look to show him he was *not* going to get to her. Even if his square jaw and chiseled features, sandy-brown hair and incredibly buff physique were permanently imprinted on her brain. She smiled sweetly. "Well, when people get to know me and realize I'm there to help, they usually become quite warm and friendly."

He surveyed her pleasantly. "That's exactly what I hope will happen between you and me. Now that we're older and wiser, that is."

Mitzy glared. She and Chase had crashed and burned once—spectacularly. There was no way she was doing it again.

He stepped closer, inundating her with his wildly intoxicating scent. "Mitzy, come on. You've been ducking my calls for weeks now."

So what? "I know it's hard for a carefree bachelor like you to understand, but I've been 'a little busy' since giving birth to quadruplets."

He shrugged. "Word around town is you've had *plenty* of volunteer help. Plus the high-end nannies your mother sent from Dallas."

Mitzy groaned and clapped a hand across her forehead.

"Didn't work out?"

"No," she bit out. "Just like this lobbying effort on your part won't work, either."

"Look, I know you'd rather not do business with me," he said, even more gently. "But at least hear me out."

Don't miss
The Texas Cowboy's Quadruplets
by Cathy Gillen Thacker.

Available October 2018 wherever
Harlequin® Special Edition books and ebooks are sold.

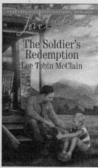

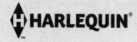